'You think I'd tell you for money?'

'Isn't that how you operate?' Ryan challenged tersely. 'Money for information. You've already accepted once, so you can't suddenly tell me my money isn't good enough.'

'I'll never think anything that comes from you is good,' she told him bluntly.

There was a speculative gleam in Ryan's eye at that. 'Nothing?' he taunted. 'Not even my kisses?'

Dear Reader

Well, summer is almost upon us. Time to think about holidays, perhaps? Where to go? What to do? And how to get everything you own into one suitcase! Wherever you decide to go, don't forget to pack plenty of Mills & Boon novels. This month's selection includes such exotic locations as Andalucía, Brazil and the Aegean Islands, so you can enjoy lots of holiday romance even if you stay at home!

The Editor

Amanda Browning still lives in the Essex house where she was born. The third of four children—her sister being her twin—she enjoyed the rough and tumble of life with two brothers as much as she did reading books. Writing came naturally as an outlet for a fertile imagination. The love of books led her to a career in libraries, and being single allowed her to take the leap into writing for a living. Success is still something of a wonder, but allows her to indulge in hobbies as varied as embroidery and bird-watching.

Recent titles by the same author:

AN OLD ENCHANTMENT
SAVAGE DESTINY

ENEMY WITHIN

BY

AMANDA BROWNING

MILLS & BOON

MILLS & BOON LIMITED
ETON HOUSE, 18-24 PARADISE ROAD
RICHMOND, SURREY TW9 1SR

All the characters in this book have no existence outside the imagination of the Author, and have no relation whatsoever to anyone bearing the same name or names. They are not even distantly inspired by any individual known or unknown to the Author, and all the incidents are pure invention.

All Rights Reserved. The text of this publication or any part thereof may not be reproduced or transmitted in any form or by any means, electronic or mechanical, including photocopying, recording, storage in an information retrieval system, or otherwise, without the written permission of the publisher.

This book is sold subject to the condition that it shall not, by way of trade or otherwise, be lent, resold, hired out or otherwise circulated without the prior consent of the publisher in any form of binding or cover other than that in which it is published and without a similar condition including this condition being imposed on the subsequent purchaser.

*First published in Great Britain 1994
by Mills & Boon Limited*

© Amanda Browning 1994

*Australian copyright 1994
Philippine copyright 1994
This edition 1994*

ISBN 0 263 78500 9

*Set in Times Roman 10 on 11 pt.
01-9406-59291 C*

Made and printed in Great Britain

CHAPTER ONE

MICKEY HANLON experienced a dismayingly familiar tightening of her stomach muscles as, through the window of what they laughingly called her office, she watched a tall male figure climbing out of a now stationary jeep. Only moments before, the vehicle had raced down the fortunately deserted track which led to the bay on which her charter business was situated, leaving a slowly settling cloud of dust in its wake. With blatant disregard for the signs, he had parked in a no parking area, and Mickey knew instinctively that this was the way he went through life, obeying only the rules he wanted to, and making up the rest.

She also knew, with a faint sinking feeling, that he just had to be Ryan Douglas, the man who had chartered her float plane, and her skills, for the next few days, and for whom she had been waiting with increasing annoyance these past two hours. Justifiable annoyance, because on the telephone Ryan Douglas's secretary had been most insistent she be there to meet him. Not that that had been hard to arrange, for, with the end of summer, the chartered sightseeing trips were virtually over, although there would always be the out-of-season trade. But it had meant turning over one of her flights to another of her pilots, who should have had the day off.

She doubted she would have done it for anyone else, but there was a great deal of clout to be gained from piloting a world-famous photographer on one of his now legendary field trips. She'd caught an exhibition once while on a trip south to Vancouver, but all she knew of

5

him came from overhearing the drooling conversation
of two women who had also been visiting the show. He
was, she had discovered, in his mid-thirties and un-
married, but that hadn't impressed her half as much as
his work. There was poetry in the photographs, a vision
of a world the way it could be, even in the midst of
turmoil and carnage.

To be even peripherally involved in the production of
such art had helped her decide it would be good business
to be adaptable. Besides, there was no point in wearing
blinkers. The company desperately needed the kudos the
assignment would bring. The recession was hitting her,
too, creating a definite cash-flow problem. Keeping a
fleet of float planes in tiptop condition took a great deal
of money, and had priority, so other areas suffered. The
buildings needed urgent attention, which meant they
needed paying customers, but paying customers didn't
use a company which had all the signs of rampant seedi-
ness. Ryan Douglas was a way out of her difficulties,
and so she had made a point of being on the ground at
the specified time, only to find herself kicking her heels
uselessly.

Now the root cause of her irritability was walking towards the converted boat shed as if he hadn't a care in
the world. A leather flying jacket sat comfortably on
broad shoulders, while a pair of long legs, encased in
thigh-hugging jeans, ate up the ground in loping strides.
The ease with which he carried a canvas grip hinted at
latent power, a power not solely allied to mere physical
strength. Here was a man who was in complete control
of himself and his life, and for no accountable reason
Mickey shivered, the tiny hairs standing up all over her
body.

He made her feel threatened, in a way she had thought
long buried, consigned to the very recesses of her brain
with all other memories of Jean-Luc. She shuddered at
the name, lips thinning, and thrust the memory away,

concentrating on the present walking towards her. She wished she could see his face, but that was hidden in the shadow cast by the peak of his slouch hat. Faces told you a great deal about a person—whether they laughed a lot, and if they were to be trusted. She'd learnt that much from past mistakes, and wasn't about to forget it. Unfortunately there was no chance to see this one, for three strides later he had disappeared into the building, leaving her with a feeling of edginess that bordered on tension.

At which point she got a firm grip on herself. She had no time to be so femininely fanciful. Jean-Luc was in the past. She was no longer prey to the kind of emotions he had aroused in her. If she was tense, she had every reason to be. The company which had become her life was under threat, and, added to that, she hadn't heard from her sister Leah for some time. She was being silly to worry. Leah was probably caught up in university life. Everyone knew the young were notoriously forgetful. She'd write, very contritely, when she remembered.

Mickey squared her shoulders. She was a business-woman, and was here to do a job. Running a small fleet of planes out of British Columbia had not been easy in a male-dominated field, but an unsuspected gritty determination had kept her going. She had forged a niche in life where she was liked and respected, a zillion miles away from the life she had left eight years ago, when she had been a deeply unhappy twenty-year-old. No man was going to undermine her achievements, no matter who he thought he was.

'Hey, Mac? Is Hanlon inside?' The abrupt tones of a deep male voice, coming from only yards away, broke into her reverie, making her jump and bringing an ir-ritated scowl to her face at her reaction.

'Mickey? Yep, sure.' The slightly bemused tone of Sid Meeks, her mechanic and right-hand-man, echoed across the former boat shed which served as a hangar.

Footsteps approached the office, and she turned away from the window, crossing to her desk, unconsciously bracing herself for the meeting. The door was thrust open without a preliminary knock, and an electric force seemed to explode into the room along with the man. Mickey had never experienced anything remotely like it, and perhaps that was why her words came out far more sharply than she had intended.

'You're late, Mr Douglas!' she snapped, taking an instant dislike to this male who seemed to think he could arrogantly do anything he liked. She had met the sort before. Jean-Luc had been a prime example, and her experiences with him had opened her eyes with a vengeance. Such men were anathema to her, and if she had known beforehand what this man was like she would never have agreed to spend an hour with him, let alone a few days!

At the sound of her voice the focus of her attention stopped abruptly; then, to her surprise and chagrin, he laughed, a deep-throated sound which almost curled her toes even as she tensed angrily. As her cheeks turned pink he propped his shoulder against the doorpost, tipped his hat on to the back of his head, and gave out with a long, soundless whistle.

She could see all she wanted of his face then. He had impossibly long-lashed blue eyes beneath mockingly raised brows, an aquiline nose and a mouth with a sensuality that should have carried a health warning! He was quite the most handsome man she had ever seen, and she had seen enough in her short life to know the difference between this and plain good looks. This man had it all, down to the dimple in his chin. The ruggedness of his jaw stopped him from looking effeminate, which was fortunate, for beneath his hat she could see a cluster of dark curls.

All this she absorbed in seconds, plus two undeniable facts. First he seemed vaguely familiar, and secondly he found her amusing. She hadn't been prepared for the latter, nor the way his eyes began a slow inspection of her person. They didn't miss much on the way down, and any lapse was accounted for on the way up. He noted the well worn boots on her feet, the shapeless khaki cords cinched in at her waist with a wide leather belt. His eyes lingered on the red plaid shirt, then followed the crimson tide up over an elfin face entirely devoid of make-up, large green eyes flashing angrily, full lips pulled into a tight line, until finally they skipped over the close-cropped black hair crammed beneath a dusty bush hat.

Crossing his arms, he shook his head. 'What the hell are you supposed to be, a female Indiana Jones?' he queried tauntingly.

Even Mickey, who rarely went to the cinema, had heard of the character he named, and she knew the reference was meant as no compliment, spoken the way it was. He found her lacking. Amusing in a pitiful way. To her surprise, considering the view was hardly novel, from this man she found she didn't like it, not one little bit.

'I didn't dress to please you, Mr Douglas!'

That enticing mouth curved. 'Nor any man, I shouldn't imagine. What's the matter? Don't you like being a woman, or are you just scared of being one?' he mocked back immediately.

To her everlasting dismay, her reaction was disgustingly feminine. 'How dare you? You're the rudest man I've ever met!' she exclaimed furiously.

Mickey had never received such open scorn before. She was intelligent enough to realise her style of dress was considered odd, but she didn't care. Her clothes were asexual, and that was exactly the way she wanted it. How typical of a man to assume that because she didn't wear clothes which advertised her as 'available' she had to be scared! Well, she wasn't advertising because she had nothing for sale. She had opted out. No doubt he would

see that as unnatural, whereas she had merely taken
control of her life, refusing to be at the mercy of her
own hormones. She was not a body, but a person, and
as a person she did not need to advertise her sex.

Far from being repentant, Ryan Douglas merely made
himself more comfortable, crossing his long legs at the
ankles. 'Is that so? Well, you're sure the strangest woman
I've ever met,' he said conversationally.

Entirely forgetting that it was bad business to alienate
a paying customer, especially one so desperately needed,
she felt acid fly to her tongue. 'And you've known so
many, I suppose?'

Ryan Douglas grinned. 'Only my fair share. How
about you?'

Mickey's eyes narrowed as she detected the way the
conversation was turning. How like a man to see her
only as a sex object! And not a very alluring one at that!
Her chin lifted belligerently. 'How about me, what?'

If her direct challenge was meant to halt him, it failed
signally. 'How many men have you known?' he enlarged
obligingly, making her wish she'd kept her mouth shut.

'One too many,' she retorted snappily, and experienced an odd sensation in her stomach when his lips
parted in a broad smile as he laughed.

'Ouch! The...lady...has got claws all right! You've
got looks too. Have you always done your best to play
them down, or did something happen to send you into
hiding?'

His choice of words was staggering, and without
warning she was plunged into the black pit of remem-
brance, seeing Jean-Luc's face as he laughed at her and
told her she was a fool. Sexy, but a fool. The vision
disappeared as she shivered and found herself back in
the present. For a moment she could only stare at Ryan
Douglas in a kind of shock, thinking, How on earth
could he know? The answer came quickly: he couldn't.
It had been a lucky taunt, and only her reaction was in

danger of revealing what she had kept so carefully hidden.

In an instant, shock turned to an icy hauteur she hadn't used in years. 'Mr Douglas, I suggest you mind your own business,' she told him coldly. 'And while you're about it, you might as well turn around and go back where you came from.' Hang the consequences; there was no way—absolutely no way—she would do business with this man!

He didn't like her tone, or her suggestion; that was certain. The relaxation left him. 'Lady, I don't know who you are, but if you're supposed to be some outlandish excuse for a secretary why don't you do your job and get Hanlon for me?' Looking around the sparsely furnished room, his eyes narrowed sharply, before shooting back to her. 'I was told he was in here. Where is he? Hiding?'

There was something less than casual in the tone of that one word, but Mickey was too wrathful to pick it up. It gave her intense pleasure to cross her arms and raise her own eyebrows mockingly. 'You're looking right at him, Mr Douglas.' An outlandish excuse for a secretary? He had some nerve!

Ryan Douglas froze, a deep frown cutting into his forehead as he swiftly shook his head. 'Uh-uh. Sorry, sweetheart, but that's where you're wrong. I'm talking about Michael Hanlon, the owner of this business, and he's very much a man.'

Again there was an undercurrent which she only registered peripherally. Her thoughts were on what a joy it was to put his charming nose out of joint. 'I'm sorry to disappoint you, but I'm afraid it's you who are mistaken, Mr Douglas,' she countered with a sweet smile.

Blue eyes hardened with a suspicion of anger. 'There's no way on earth you can be Michael Hanlon.'

'Not Michael, Mr Douglas, Michaela, but my *friends* call me Mickey. Would you care to see my passport?'

she returned smoothly, once more in control, and enjoying his discomfiture. She suspected it wasn't very often that anyone got the better of this man.

Ryan Douglas swore, violently. 'The hell you say! All your company details, right down to your letterheading, refer to Michael Hanlon as the owner. How do you explain that, or can I do it myself? Is that the way you usually get work, by hiding the fact that you're a woman and cheating your way into a job?'

The unjust allegation made her blood boil. The truth was she had used the last of the correctly headed stationery some time ago, and as there hadn't been the spare cash to order more she had latched on to the idea of using her father's, as the difference was only one letter. It was her custom to ink in an 'a', but this time she must have forgotten to do so. She was left on the defensive, which she hated. 'A printing error,' she lied blithely, before getting on to the nitty-gritty. 'For your information I didn't hide the fact that I'm a woman, and I've certainly never lied my way into a job!'

An icy gaze gave her the once-over again. 'From where I'm standing you're doing your best to make yourself sexless!'

Clearly he meant the words to sting, but Mickey only felt vindicated in her choice. She had no desire to be the focus of anyone's attention, and especially not a man's. No, she had lived in the spotlight, experienced its notoriety, and now all she wanted to do was fade into the background with the rest of humanity. That wasn't too much to ask, surely? Not the crime he made it out to be!

'However,' he went on tersely, 'it makes no difference, honey, because it's a well known fact that I never work with women.'

She just bet he didn't! Women had other uses! As the scornful thoughts whipped through her brain, she suddenly recalled why he had seemed so familiar. She'd read an article at the dentist's about a man they'd labelled a 'connoisseur of women'. Disgusted, she hadn't bothered to notice the man's name, but now she realised the picture had been of Ryan Douglas. And connoisseur was just the word, because, although he didn't photograph them, he certainly appreciated their beauty. He always had them around him, and working was far from his mind!

She didn't know whom she despised most, the women who let themselves be used, or the man who did the using!

Her lips pursed, angered by his cutting remarks and his blatant chauvinism. If there was one thing Mickey knew implicitly, it was her ability to do her job. 'My sex doesn't come into it, only my competence. If you'd bothered to ask, anyone could have told you I was female. In fact, I assumed you knew. However, you needn't worry about compromising your chauvinistic pride, because this is one woman you certainly won't be working with!' And with that declaration she bent down to pick up a tan flying jacket, so similar to his own, which lay by the desk.

Which was as far as she got, because, when she turned, Ryan Douglas's large frame blocked her exit. Involuntarily she reared back a step, eyes sending out icy darts, even as her brain registered the shock-wave of heat which had seemed to flow from him, and the tangy scent of his aftershave. 'Excuse me,' she said pointedly, hands tightening on the leather in automatic rejection of the way her senses had rioted in response.

Dear lord, the very last thing she had ever expected or wanted was to be attracted to this man! But she knew herself now, recognising the singing rush of blood through her veins had nothing to do with loathing. The thought brought with it a sickening self-contempt. Scornfully she asked herself why she should be surprised. He was just like Jean-Luc, a user, and heaven knew her weakness there! Would she never learn?

'And just where the hell do you think you're going?' he demanded tersely.

Mickey ground her teeth, grateful for a fresh surge of dislike. 'If you'll just get out of the way, I'm leaving, which will please both of us no end!' she returned pithily.

One long arm reached out, his hand closing on her arm and cutting off the blood. 'Oh, no, you don't! I hired you, and I sure haven't fired you.'

She tried to pull free, alarmed to feel the imprint of each finger and the warmth of his palm, but he foiled the attempt with ease, which only made her angrier. 'A formality, surely. After all, like it or not, I am a woman, and you don't like them if they have brains, do you, Mr Douglas?' she scorned.

His hold relaxed slightly, and a lazy warmth entered his eyes, deepening the blue to mysterious depths. 'Oh, I like all sorts of women. At least, women who look like women. I simply don't work with them because they're trouble. They always try to mix business with pleasure.'

Dear God, the man was insufferable, and if she kept thinking that way the fledgling attraction would wither and die. 'Meaning you think you're irresistible? Well, here's one woman who disagrees!'

'But then you're not a real woman, are you, Mickey Hanlon?' he taunted softly, and she paled, her breath catching at the unexpectedly sharp dart of pain which shot through her.

It took a real effort to hold his gaze and not reveal just how he had got to her. By 'real woman', no doubt he meant some mindless sex object, and that she refused to be ever again. 'Whatever my supposed failings, I'll be taking them with me when I go.' Which couldn't be soon enough as far as she was concerned.

'And just where am I going to get another pilot at such short notice?' Ryan Douglas ground out harshly.

Of all the arrogant...! He thought he could say what he liked and still get her co-operation. Not this time.

'That's your problem. You made the rules. No women, remember? So goodbye, Mr Douglas.' When she tugged at her arm again, she found herself instantly released. However, the sense of freedom was fleeting.

'Leave here, and I'll sue you for breach of contract.'

The threat halted her in the doorway, and she turned swiftly. He was smiling, but the smile on his lips failed to reach his eyes, and she shivered atavistically. 'You can't be serious?'

He laughed drily. 'I've never been more so.'

Mickey took a steadying breath. If ever there was a time for caution, this was it. 'But you don't want me,' she pointed out, then mentally kicked herself as she realised how unfortunate the statement was.

It wasn't lost on him. One sardonic eyebrow rose. 'An apt choice of words. Unfortunately, time is short, and if you're the owner of this...establishment, then it has to be you I deal with,' he declared grimly, mouth hardening into an indomitable line.

While common sense was telling Mickey she should get out of there as fast as her legs could carry her, she knew his threat was far from just talk. While it was unnerving, she was brought up short with a reminder that she was reacting most unprofessionally. She had never walked out on a job yet, but, more than that, she couldn't risk her whole livelihood so recklessly. Though it galled her to do it, she curbed her dislike. 'What are you suggesting? That I put one of my male pilots at your disposal?' she challenged, determined to be as professional as she knew how.

A devilish amusement quirked at his lips, but a glance at his eyes would have shown them to be as hard as diamonds. 'The contract specifically states that M. Hanlon is to be my pilot. That being the case, I'm prepared to overlook the fact that you're a woman. After all, you're doing your best to pretend you aren't one. And I've a feeling you'll agree to the compromise, because you think

you're a match for any man, don't you, Mickey—short
for Michaela—Hanlon?'

There were good reasons for Mickey's chosen lifestyle, but that wasn't one of them. Not that she was
about to explain herself to this man. 'I'm a professional,
Mr Douglas. That's why you hired me, and that's what
you'll get. However, I may have signed a contract with
you, but it doesn't give you the right to throw insults at
me all day long,' she protested, determined to set some
ground rules here and now.

Taking off his hat, Ryan Douglas raked a hand
through his hair. 'You'll have to learn to develop a thick
skin to go with the trousers if you want to be taken
seriously, Hanlon,' he observed drily, before settling the
hat back more comfortably. 'OK, now you'd better show
me round.'

She had been just about to protest the scathing use of
her surname, but his command halted the flow. This was
something she hadn't taken into consideration. She had
no reason to be ashamed of her fleet, although two of
her float planes were temporarily out of commission,
waiting for spares—which also cost money, so that they
were seriously considering cannibalising one to keep the
others air-worthy. And there was no denying that the
adapted boat shed had seen better days. Even the sign
was faded and flaking.

'Is that absolutely necessary?' she queried stiffly,
knowing that an outright refusal would only make him
suspect she had something far more serious to hide than
bad paintwork.

A fact not lost on him as he stared her out. 'Is there
any reason why I shouldn't take a look?'

A reason other than that she disliked him intensely?
'None at all,' she said coldly, and led the way out with
head held high.

There was not much to see, and she showed him round
both inside and out on the jetty with her back ramrod-

straight. It didn't help to view her property through his eyes, noticing where several boards needed replacing here, or a coat of paint was needed there. For an instant she wished she had asked Leah for a loan after all, but knew the reasons for not doing so hadn't changed. Just because someone had money, it didn't mean you had the right to ask for some of it, even if they were your family.

Recalling that made her wonder once again what Leah was doing. It was unlike her not to have been in touch, and she made a mental note to write to Sophie the minute she got home tonight.

A sharp question brought her back to her major problem, and, biting back the urge to defend the depressingly seedy look of things, Mickey kept her observations brief and to the point. She knew that where it counted, namely the float planes, everything was in good order. Sid regularly serviced each machine, just as he was now doing to hers. For his part, Ryan Douglas said little, merely took everything in non-committally. Only when they had returned to the office did he turn a poker face her way.

'Right, I've seen enough; let's go.'

Having been expecting a scathing indictment of her company, Mickey was taken aback. 'Go? Go where?'

That pitying look she was fast coming to loathe returned to his face. 'To dinner, of course. I've just had one hell of a journey, and I'm tired and hungry. I'm booked into the Crest Motor Hotel, so we'll eat there.'

His assumption that she would simply fall in with whatever plan he chose was like waving a red rag. Once she might have slavishly obeyed any order Jean-Luc had given, but those days were long gone. When you rediscovered self-worth, you didn't abandon it again to anyone! Mickey quickly counted to ten before exploding. 'Oh, we will, will we? Let me remind you, Mr Douglas, you hired a pilot, not a dinner companion!'

'Just as well I did, because there's nothing more liable to put me off my food than sitting across from a sour-faced woman.'

Mickey gasped in outrage. 'Your charm overwhelms me!'

His gaze became speculative. 'Do you want me to charm you, Hanlon? I thought you wanted me to treat you like a man.'

'I want...' She stopped her hasty retort mid-flow, aware that she was only making herself ridiculous in his eyes.

'Yes? You want...?' Ryan Douglas prompted, the glint of laughter in his eyes confirming her thought.

Mickey drew breath slowly, amazed at how easily her usual calm temperament had been changed to aggression by the man standing before her. And as that only appeared to amuse him, she'd be civil if it killed her. 'Mr Douglas, it's been a long, frustrating day for me, too. All I want to do is go home.'

If she had hoped to appeal to a better side of his nature, she quickly discovered he didn't have one. 'Your wants will have to wait. There are certain matters which have to be discussed. I didn't plan on dealing with a woman, but nothing else has changed. We'll have our...talk...over dinner.'

Mickey fumed inwardly. He could have told her that in the first place, but he'd been having too much fun goading her. Though she was ready to spit nails, she found a dignified reply. 'Very well, Mr Douglas, if you insist.'

'Oh, I do,' he returned softly. 'And I also insist you stop calling me Mr Douglas. My name is Ryan; use it.'

Not a request, but a command. Well, two could play at that game. 'And my name is Mickey, not Hanlon!'

He had the gall to grin. 'Hanlon suits you better. Mickey is soft and feminine, while Hanlon is as tough as old boots.'

If she had had an old boot, she would have chucked it right at his grinning face! What *had* she let herself in for? Even a day in Ryan Douglas's company would be pure purgatory. But perhaps there was a way she could get a little of her own back. After all, they were on the ground now, but in the air they were in her territory. She'd find out then just what sort of stuff Ryan Douglas was made of!

She looked up to find those intense blue eyes had narrowed. 'Stop looking like the cat who got the cream, Hanlon. You're beginning to make me nervous.'

Mickey swallowed back a caustic laugh. The man didn't have a nerve in the whole of his body! 'We wouldn't want that, would we, Mr...*Ryan*?' She stressed his name as she caught the lift of his brows. 'Not when you're putting your life in my hands.' She waggled her fingers under his nose, and very nearly yelped when he caught hold of them in his own large, strong hand. She couldn't have protested even if she'd wanted to, because the jolt of electricity which had shot up her arm at the contact took her breath away. Horrified, she found herself staring at the sight of her own slim hand imprisoned in his, while her heart thudded almost painfully in her chest.

Meanwhile, Ryan was studying his captive. 'Hmm, long, graceful fingers. Hardly the strong, practical type. Are you sure you're in the right line of work? Somehow, they just don't fit the image,' he mused, and Mickey quickly snatched her hand away, grateful for the excuse.

'Don't worry, I haven't lost a paying passenger...yet,' she shot back with all the aplomb she could muster, while surreptitiously rubbing her hand down her trousers in an attempt to stop the tingling.

His lips quirked. 'I don't like the way you said that. Could you, by any chance, be flirting with me, Hanlon?'

She froze, the animation dying out of her face. She couldn't—wouldn't—flirt with him, for to do so would be flirting with danger. Mentally and physically, she backed off. 'Hardly! Women like me don't flirt with men like you,' she enlarged with distaste.

'You say that as if you've met men like me before. Was it one of them who sent you running?' he queried shrewdly, but only managed to put her on an even keel again.

Secure in the knowledge that men like him and Jean-Luc were too vain to see they might not be the be-all and end-all, Mickey curved her lips with icy amusement. 'Strange, isn't it, how men always imagine it must be one of their kind who makes a woman the way she is?'

'That's because it usually is,' Ryan observed watch-fully. 'You're saying you're different?'

She laughed, turning to the door once more. 'I'm not saying anything.' She refused to be drawn into a personal discussion with him.

Ryan followed her out into the hangar. 'You don't need to, Hanlon; your silence speaks for you.'

Unseen by her antagonist, Mickey briefly closed her eyes. 'Back off, Ryan. You're my passenger, not my confessor.'

Behind her, he laughed. 'Do you have anything to confess?' he challenged, then came to an abrupt halt as she swung to face him.

He had pushed her an inch too far, and her finger stabbed at his chest. 'If you want a confession, here's one. I've made mistakes in my life, but the biggest one was having anything to do with you!'

Hands hooked into the belt loops of his jeans, he looked down at her mockingly. 'Why so touchy? Have I hit a nerve or ten?'

Mickey turned away in a movement that was distress-ingly nearly a flounce. 'Not even close. I just got out of bed the wrong side this morning,' she snapped, trying to recover lost ground.

'If you'd been in it with a man, it wouldn't matter what side you got out of,' he sent after her, bringing her round again, cheeks flaming.

Painful memories rose dangerously near the surface, of reckless, selfish taking. But nothing was free. Pleasure had to be paid for. Passion could be a curse, a greedy monster. 'Sex isn't the answer to everything!' she spluttered angrily.

For once Ryan didn't laugh. 'If it isn't the cure, it's often the cause.'

Mickey was beginning to feel she was being put through an emotional wringer, and every time she tried to free herself she just went round again. 'Thank you, Dr Freud, and goodnight. For someone who says he won't work with a woman, you keep harping on the fact that I am one,' she accused.

'Just trying to figure out what makes you tick, Hanlon,' Ryan answered smoothly.

'Better men than you have tried, and failed in the attempt,' she shot back, and regretted it immediately when his lips curved drily.

'Froze them all off, did you? I can't say that surprises me. So it shouldn't surprise you to hear you might just have met your match,' he observed softly, with an undertone which set her heart knocking.

Alarm shot through her system before she could suppress it. 'You're forgetting your own rules, Ryan,' she reminded him, far too breathlessly. She felt vulnerable, and it was a bad feeling, because she knew the enemy was as much within as without.

'Ah, but then rules are made to be broken. You intrigue me, Hanlon, and that means you might just be worth making an exception of.'

CHAPTER TWO

THE Crest Motor Hotel was a well known landmark in Prince Rupert, sitting on its bluff overlooking the harbour. Mickey had only ever admired it in passing. Entering the lobby, dressed in working clothes as she still was, made her feel that all eyes turned her way. Lord, how she hated that sensation! It plunged her back into another time, when every move she made had drawn avid attention, when she had felt the sting of shame burning her flesh and it had been as if a scarlet 'A' had been emblazoned on her forehead.

She had done everything she could to make sure that would never happen to her again, down to wearing non-feminine clothes, and yet, with a feeling of almost hysterical irony, she found herself once again the centre of attention. What was everyone thinking? That she and this handsome, incredibly sexy man were going upstairs to...? She battened down hard on the thought. She was getting paranoid. It was guilt talking. Guilt because she couldn't ignore the attraction she felt. But only she knew that; everyone else was probably thinking she looked a mess!

Shakily she adjourned the mental court inside her brain which constantly sat in judgement of herself. Yes, it was her appearance which caused comment, and for the first time in years she regretted leaving her designer clothes behind. Tonight she could have done with the boost to her confidence that a fashionable suit would have provided.

As she followed in Ryan's wake, paradoxically comforted by the thought, she quite missed the fact that the reason people turned to look was because of the natural pride and confidence in her bearing.

Ryan's suite was on the top floor, above the hustle and bustle of the town, and walking into it was like entering a haven of peace. For all of thirty seconds. It took that long for Mickey to walk inside, take an appreciative look at the comfortable furnishings, and turn round. Whereupon she had the fortune, or misfortune, to be in time to see Ryan Douglas turn the key in the lock, before removing and pocketing it securely. The shock had her eyes swinging to his face to meet an expression so grim that her stomach lurched.

'What are you doing?' The question came out in a husky waver, and, dismayed to sound so wishy-washy, she dredged up enough steel to add demandingly, 'Why have you locked us in?'

He chose not to answer immediately. Removing his hat and coat and tossing them on to a chair, Ryan strode menacingly towards her, halting almost painfully close. 'Not us, Hanlon, just you. We have some talking to do, and I don't want you running away.'

The statement was hardly designed to ease the erratic thumping of her heart. She had no idea what was going on, but she didn't like it anyway. It was hard not to think of all those scary tales of kidnapping, but she told herself this was Ryan Douglas, not some thug. All the same, she was determined to camouflage her growing tension at finding herself in the midst of this new and startling situation.

'Isn't this a little extreme for talking over flight plans?' she attempted to joke, while looking for a means of escape. It didn't take long to realise they were too high up for there to be any safer exit than the door.

A fact Ryan was fully aware of, and, although he had taken the precaution of locking the door, he still kept himself between her and it. Moreover, he didn't laugh. 'Cut out the chit-chat and just tell me where they are,' he commanded, in a voice which could have shattered rock at twenty paces.

If she'd hoped for instant enlightenment, at his words the darkness only deepened. Completely at a loss, she stared at him, deciding he was utterly mad, and wondering why nobody else had ever noticed it. Hadn't someone once said the way to handle madmen was to humour them? It seemed to her to be a wise course.

She manufactured a faintly questioning smile. 'You'll have to tell me more than that. Where are what? What exactly are you talking about?' she queried with as much concern as she could muster.

It went down like a ton of bricks. An angry hand slashed through the air, cutting her off so abruptly that she flinched. 'You know damn well!'

Mickey struggled to make sense of it all. She could feel an incredible anger coming at her in waves. She had never experienced such violent animosity before, not even when the news of her involvement with Jean-Luc had broken, making her the butt of universal condemnation. All at once her knees began to tremble, and her heart to race. This sounded like trouble with a capital 'T', and she couldn't even begin to defend herself until she knew the reason. So she had to continue fighting in the dark.

'All I know is that you're crazy! You lure me here under false pretences, lock me in, and then make irrational demands! Whatever you're looking for, I haven't got it!' It was good to feel angry, for it smothered her anxiety.

Ryan moved like lightning to catch her by the shoulders and shake her roughly. 'God, I should have known you'd be bloody perverse. You're in it too, aren't you? Right up to your sweet little neck!'

Though nothing made sense, when danger threatened Mickey acted instinctively. Her foot lashed out, the heavy boot connecting with his shin with a highly satisfactory thunk, and as he yelped and released her she had the presence of mind to quickly put herself out of range beyond the couch. From there she watched him rub his sore leg briefly before straightening to glare at her. She held up a faintly trembling hand to keep him at bay.

'Stay right where you are, or, so help me, I'll scream blue murder!' she threatened, fully prepared to carry it out.

Ryan Douglas's broad chest rose and fell sharply as he took a breath. He stayed where he was, but not because he was afraid of scandal, simply because it suited him better. Mickey swallowed nervously to moisten a mouth which had taken on the aspect of a particularly arid desert. Clearly he was battling a compulsive urge to throttle her, and it appeared to take a great effort for him to sound reasonable.

'There's no need for you to scream. If you don't want to prolong this unpleasant interview, just tell me where Peter is... where they both are.'

There he went again! Did he think she was crazy too? If she had known she would have told him, just to get out of there. Unfortunately, Mickey was as much in the dark as ever. 'Who is Peter, and who are "they"?' she demanded helplessly, with predictable results.

Those incredible blue eyes narrowed. 'You know, this pretence of ignorance is doing nothing for my patience, Hanlon,' he said testily, then breathed in deeply. 'OK, OK, if it will get me some answers I'll go along with it. But be warned, my patience isn't endless. Peter is Peter Douglas, my nephew.'

He could have said Rip Van Winkle for all the relevance it had to her. 'Is that supposed to convey something?' Edgily, she knew what reaction her response would receive.

His jaw clenched. 'You're darn right it should, because Peter is the man your precious sister has got her gold-digging claws into!'

Mickey was stunned. Of all the answers she might have imagined, that had never occurred to her. 'Leah?' An awful foreboding clenched her heart as she recalled her own concern over the lack of communication with her sister.

At her mention of the name, a grim smile twisted his lips. 'So you haven't forgotten everything,' he drawled nastily. 'Yes, Leah. Your scheming sister has got Peter so besotted, he's run off with her! But let me tell you something: if she thinks she's got a meal-ticket for life, she's got another think coming!'

Shock rapidly gave way to anger, which welled up like a volcanic eruption. 'Hold it! Who do you think you're calling a gold-digger?' she challenged violently, seeing in her mind's eye the sweet face of her young half-sister. Gold-digger? If anything, Leah was quite dismayingly unworldly.

'What else would you call a woman who convinces a man to run off with her after five minutes' acquaintance?'

She didn't fully understand the situation, but she knew Leah was under attack, and that was enough. Like a tigress coming to the defence of her young, Mickey balled her hands into fists. 'Don't you dare say another word, Ryan Douglas, because you've got hold of the wrong girl. My sister Leah has not run away with anyone. She's studying for her degree at university.' True enough, but that niggle of doubt increased. Why hadn't Leah been in touch?

An eyebrow rose mockingly. 'Really? Well, believe it or not, she's found a new career,' he sneered.

The gibe brought an angry growl to her throat. 'Well, I don't believe you! Leah hasn't mentioned anyone to me. I know my sister, and deceit is beyond her. I don't know this Peter, but, if he's anything like you, then it's my belief that any seducing has been done by your own precious nephew!' Mickey charged back fiercely, rounding the couch to square up to him.

'Peter isn't the one who needs money. He has enough of his own, as if you didn't know!' he put in caustically.

Mickey felt ready to explode. 'I *don't* know, and Leah doesn't need money either!' She had inherited a considerable sum from both her mother and her father, and could expect vastly more from her grandmother.

Ryan remained distinctly unimpressed by her avowal. 'That isn't the impression I got from looking around your business this afternoon. If I've ever seen a building in urgent need of repair, then that was it!' He laughed derisively.

Hot colour washed in and out of her cheeks. 'Damn you, Leah has nothing to do with my business! Which doesn't need your money either, just a fresh coat of paint and a nail or two! I've been waiting for the time, and the money, to do the repairs,' she lied bravely, only to see his lip curl.

'Do you take me for a fool? Do you think I didn't have your financial status checked out? You're barely keeping your head above water, Hanlon. If your sister has money, which I doubt, then it isn't in the quantity you need. Only a large slice of the Douglas fortune is going to bail you out!'

Mickey paled at the knowledge of just how much he knew about her lack of funds, but it didn't alter one basic fact. 'If you say I need the money, then why are you calling Leah the gold-digger?' she demanded hoarsely.

The look in his eyes wasn't flattering. 'Who would fall under your spell, Hanlon? You needed Leah to bait the trap, and, once you'd caught Peter, your loving sister would hand over all that lovely money to you!'

Her colour rose with her chin. 'It sounds very plausible, but you're wrong on every count! There is no plot—at least, not with my family. I don't know how you came by your erroneous information, but, whoever your nephew has run off with, it certainly isn't my sister,' she protested hardily.

Ryan watched her closely for a moment, as if deciding whether he could get away with what he would really like to do, then swung on his heel and went to pour himself a drink. 'Tell me, did your father have more than one daughter named Leah?'

Never taking her eyes off him for a moment, Mickey crossed her arms defensively. 'Of course not! But the name Leah is hardly uncommon. Why pick on us?'

Draining a glass of whisky, he walked back to her. 'Because that was the name Peter gave in his letter. However, as I don't expect you to believe me, you can read it for yourself.' He produced the missive from his shirt pocket, rather like a conjurer.

She accepted the letter, but held it as if it might bite her. However, after reading only the first paragraph, Mickey slowly sank down on to the couch, and started from the top. Whoever Peter was, the girl he described certainly *sounded* like her sister—A black-haired, dark-eyed angel, who loved him for himself. But he knew his uncle wouldn't approve, so they were going away together. Nobody was to worry; they would come back when they were ready. There was more in the same vein. When she reached the end, Mickey looked up at the now silent man who stood before her.

The heat of anger had died out of her, leaving her, for the moment, uncertain. She clung to the rug, lest it be pulled completely out from under her feet. 'There has to be some mistake. Leah would never just run off like that!' She wouldn't not get in touch either, but you know she hasn't, Mickey told herself silently.

'You know her so well?'

Considering she hadn't even known of her sibling's existence until eight years ago, Mickey deemed it wisest not to answer that, even though, in her heart, her answer would have been an emphatic yes. 'You're wrong. I know you are. Leah is at the university,' she declared with all the assurance she could muster. If she could use the phone, she'd prove it.

Ryan dropped another bombshell. 'No, she isn't. She hasn't shown up for classes for the past three weeks.'

The absolute conviction in his voice was enough to startle Mickey. 'Three weeks!' she exclaimed in dismay, wishing she could argue, but knowing this, at least, had to be true. Because he could only have found out by checking with the faculty.

Ryan, on the other hand, derived no such certainty from her tone. 'Do you really expect me to believe you didn't know?'

She glared at him, having had more than enough of his vile accusations regarding both herself and her sister. 'If you think I'd calmly sit by while my sister ruined her life, you're very much mistaken!' Three weeks! Exactly the length of time since Leah had last called her! Surely her sister couldn't have done anything so foolish as to run off with a strange man?

Ryan snorted disgustedly. 'Hardly ruined. Peter must be worth half a million dollars at the last count. Not that he can get his hands on it until he's twenty-five, which might not amuse your sister at all. I imagine she's been having a whale of a time deciding just how she'll spend it.'

At that, Mickey shot to her feet, thrusting the crumpled letter back at him. 'I refuse to listen to any more of this! If Leah isn't at the university, then she's with her grandmother.' That had to be the explanation. She just knew Leah wouldn't have done any of what this vile man was suggesting. The trouble was, reference to Grandmother Sophie was hardly likely to instil unqualified confidence. Not that she'd reveal her doubts for the world! No, there was a solid-gold reason for her sister not being at the university, and she was going to find out just what it was!

However, before she could say so, her protagonist was exclaiming, 'Grandmother?' in a tone which implied she had caught him off balance for once.

Mickey couldn't hide her look of triumph. 'You didn't know about her, did you? It seems you don't know everything!'

He sent her a stony look, then marched across to the telephone. Lifting the receiver, he held it out to her. 'OK, ring her and ask her if Leah's there.'

She would have loved to—anything to rub his nose in it—but it was impossible. 'I can't. Sophie doesn't have a phone.' Wouldn't, was actually a truer word. Her eccentricities were as ever, impractical.

With a muttered oath, Ryan crashed the receiver back into the rest, and gathered up his coat. 'Then we'll go and pay her a visit. Where does she live?'

He was already slipping his arms into his jacket as her jaw dropped. 'You're crazy. She lives clear over in Kitimat. It will take ages to get there!'

For all the notice he took, she might have been saying Leah's grandmother lived on the moon. He merely proceeded to unlock the door. 'I came here with the express purpose of bringing Peter home. I have no intention of leaving without him, nor will I give you the chance to warn anyone by waiting until tomorrow!'

It was like batting her head against a brick wall. And Mickey stamped her foot in exasperation. 'Don't you listen to a word I say? I'm not involved in a conspiracy. You've been reading too many spy novels.'

Over his shoulder, his look was pitying. 'Having been found out, you'd hardly be likely to admit to anything. Of course, if what you're trying to do is keep me from discovering Leah isn't where you say she is, then I'll just draw my own conclusions.'

Mickey couldn't think how she had ever thought this man attractive! He was loathsome. Everything she said was turned around to suit his purpose. Nothing would do but to show him how wrong he was to his face. 'All right, we'll go,' she agreed grudgingly, and joined him at the door.

His smile was sardonic. 'I'm glad to see you're an intelligent woman, Hanlon.'

She sent him a daggers look. 'If I'd had any intelligence, I'd have seen you coming!'

'You'd have to get up very early in the morning to get the better of me,' he advised ironically, locking the door after them and ushering her back to the lift.

'It can't be that difficult, if your nephew managed to do it,' Mickey observed pungently.

'He hasn't got away with it yet,' he reminded her, and she pulled a face.

'How old is he?'

'Twenty-three.'

From the way his uncle had come rushing after him, she'd assumed he was much younger. 'A little old, wouldn't you say, to be kept on a leading rein?' she jeered, not surprised the young man wanted to break free.

The lift arrived, and they stepped inside before Ryan answered. 'He has his freedom, within reason.'

'The boundary of reason being the things you do or don't like,' she scorned, finding herself reluctantly empathising with the runaway.

'I'm not about to apologise for keeping him out of the clutches of female barracudas,' he informed her shortly, and took her arm as they reached the ground and headed out of the building to where the jeep had been parked earlier.

She resented being manhandled, and tried to jerk herself free, but failed once more. Grinding her teeth impotently, she found herself almost having to jog to

keep up with him. Even so, she found the breath to
protest. 'I've told you before about lumping my sister
in with such people!'

'Sorry,' he apologised mockingly, 'but I've yet to hear
anything to change my opinion. Get in.' This last came
as they reached the disreputable vehicle.

'Where did you get this—a junk heap?' she bit out
witheringly as she resisted.

'Never judge by appearances; this piece of junk is a
lot more reliable than you, sweetheart. Now are you
going to get in or...?'

Mickey only complied because she knew he would have
put her in by force if she had refused, and she wanted
to retain at least some dignity. Besides, the quickest way
of proving he was mistaken, she hoped, was to get to
Grandmother Sophie's as swiftly as possible. So she
settled into her seat without another word, and gave him
directions for leaving the town.

Once on Highway 16, her attention was only partially
on the journey; the main part of her brain became cen-
tered on Leah. When she had first come in search of her
father, she had been surprised but delighted to discover
she had a half-sister. She had known Leah for eight years
now, and loved her dearly, although she hadn't seen her
every day, because she lived with her paternal grandmother. Their father's death eighteen months ago had
been a shock to both of them. He had seemed so fit,
but he must have known he had cancer for a long time.
It had been then that her sister had decided she wanted
to study medicine.

Although they had jointly inherited the house she now
lived in, Mickey alone had inherited her father's business,
and that had helped her cope with her sense of loss. It
hadn't seemed a burden, more an acknowledgement of
her own capabilities. Although their years together had
been short, Mickey had discovered a closeness of spirit
with her father which had been totally lacking with her

mother. He had never asked her why she had abandoned the only life she had known, but she had told him anyway. He hadn't judged or advised, but had simply accepted her, and given her an unquestioning love which had gone a long way to healing her wounds. She had developed her own love of flying from being taught by her father. He had been delighted when she had gone on to show her interest in his business, and they had worked together happily, Mickey discovering a capacity for hard work into which she had channelled all her energies.

Leah had a gentler nature, although it was allied to a surprising strength of will, and a deep understanding of the frailties of her fellow humans, both of which she would need if she realised her wish to study medicine and become a doctor. It wasn't a whim, but a vocation, and that was why Mickey knew it just couldn't be Leah who had run away with Ryan's nephew. She was so dedicated, so sure of what she wanted. It would never occur to her to throw it all away on some…playboy millionaire!

'You're wrong, you know.' The statement was an extension of her thoughts, and broke the lengthy silence which had fallen.

He spared her a brief glance, and seemed to know immediately what she was referring to. 'It's for sure one of us is doomed to be disappointed,' he concurred obliquely, and Mickey found herself studying his handsome profile with resentment.

Rather late in the day, a vital point struck her. 'You never intended to take any photographs, did you?'

She caught the slight flexing of his cheeks which indicated he was smiling. 'Not this trip, although I do have plans for the future.'

His smugness was so galling! 'Wouldn't you call that breach of contract? I could sue you, too,' she declared, thinking of all the preparations which had had to be

made. The company's outlay had been quite considerable at a time when it could be ill afforded.

'I take it from your remark that you didn't read the
small print? That was careless, Hanlon,' he tutted re-
provingly, stirring the hardly settled ashes of her anger.

'Meaning?'

'Meaning I contracted to use an aircraft and pilot of
Hanlon Air "for an unspecified time". Which, roughly
translated, means if I don't use you, I don't have to pay
you.'

To his credit, he didn't sound as if he was gloating,
but she felt as furious as if he had been anyway. For she
had indeed read that clause, and had taken it to mean
the trip was open-ended. In fact she had been working
on the probability that he would need her for at least a
week, and perhaps even two. Now she knew better, and
her hatred of him grew in leaps and bounds. Because he
had to have known how she would take it, how anyone
would take it.

Although it wasn't the end of the world, the sense of
being manipulated made her feel as if it was. 'Very
clever,' she said bitterly. 'I hope you can sleep nights.'

This time he sent her a longer look, laden with scep-
ticism. 'Trying to tell me you wouldn't have used my
name as an advertisement for more trade?' he queried
softly, and she flushed, squirming a little in her seat,
even though it was common practice.

'At least it would have been honest. You can't say the
same.'

'War is a dirty business, Hanlon. Take it from one
who knows,' he returned shortly, and clearly brought
down a wall between them, concentrating on his driving.

Mickey had nothing to say either, spending the re-
mainder of the journey looking forward to seeing his
face when he was proved wrong. It was likely to be the
only satisfaction she had out of the whole fiasco. Ryan
kept to the maximum speed limit, and consequently it

took less time to reach Leah's grandmother's house than usual. The lights were on when he finally drew the jeep to a halt outside the faded elegance of the three-storey building, and Mickey wasted no time, jumping down before the vehicle had properly stopped moving and hurrying up the path to knock on the door.

Sophie Trenchard opened the door herself, her statuesque frame swathed in a colourful lounging robe. Her look of irritation changed to a broad smile when she saw who her visitor was.

'Mickey!' she greeted warmly. 'What a lovely surprise. I was in the middle of a book, and just about to throw a tantrum for being interrupted mid-flow!' she added, with a wicked grin, because her penchant for behaving less maturely than befitted her years was legendary. The grin turned to a look of intrigue when a tense and grim-faced Ryan came to stand in the light issuing from the door.

Mickey returned the hug she had been swept into, feeling quite relieved to have an erstwhile ally within call. Smiling up at the older woman, she realised with a faint qualm that Sophie had apparently taken to wearing pince-nez. 'Hello, Sophie. I've come to see Leah.'

The cheerful smile reappeared on the grey-haired lady's face and didn't flicker. 'Isn't that nice? Come in, come in.'

Mickey felt her heart surge anew, and threw Ryan an 'I told you so' look over her shoulder before stepping inside.

'Is this your new man, Mickey?' the old lady asked forthrightly, eyeing the breadth and height of her adopted granddaughter's companion with unabashed interest, while Mickey stiffened in instant rejection.

'No!' The denial shot out hurriedly as she caught a wicked glint of amusement in Ryan's eyes. 'No. This is Ryan Douglas. He's come to see Leah, too.' Reluctantly she made the necessary introductions.

'Mrs Trenchard,' Ryan greeted politely as he shook hands.

'Dear boy, call me Sophie. Mickey will tell you I'm never one to stand on ceremony. I was the despair of my family!' Sophie Trenchard invited, leading the way into a cluttered lounge.

'Will Leah be long?' Mickey asked firmly, knowing how dangerous it was to let Sophie take the conversation in an altogether different direction. She assumed her sister was out, because if Leah had been in she would have come to greet them before this. It brought a return of that small niggle of doubt to her mind.

Sophie waved an airy hand. 'She said they would come back soon. Sit, Mickey. Can I get you some coffee, Ryan? Or some brandy, perhaps? Thaddeus left some here when he went away... or was it Matthew? They were twins, you see, and I never can remember which is which,' she explained, making Mickey stare at her long and hard, because Sophie wasn't at all dippy; she just pretended she was when there was an advantage to be gained. Just what the advantage was this time, she didn't yet see.

Across the room, Ryan shook his head. 'No, thank you,' he refused with a polite smile, although his eyes narrowed.

Mickey groaned inwardly, well aware of the impression he was getting, whereas the men in question were brothers who had lodged with Sophie one summer when their family home was full to bursting. She was on the verge of pointing this out when Ryan carried on speaking.

'You say Leah isn't here?' The question was mild enough, but Mickey was aware of the steel behind the words.

Sophie dislodged a cat from an armchair and sat down, nodding wisely. 'Leah and her young man have gone away for a while, but they'll be back when they're ready,' she revealed, seemingly unaware of just what a bomb-shell she had dropped.

For a moment Mickey was totally speechless, but not so Ryan. 'Does her young man have a name?'

'Of course. Peter Douglas. Ah . . .' Suddenly she made the connection, although she wasn't in the least put out. 'Your son?'

'My nephew,' Ryan corrected grittily, and Mickey was very much aware that he was holding a monumental anger in check solely because of the older woman. She knew he was thinking there weren't just two women in-volved, but three!

'A nice boy. I like him. He has a good heart. He'll do well for our Leah,' Sophie declared with satisfaction. 'You don't find young men of his standing turning up in our neck of the woods every day of the week.'

Ryan's face became stony. 'No, indeed you don't. Only a fool would let a wealthy young man get away,' he de-clared grimly, and not very subtly.

It appeared to go right over her head, for Sophie merely blinked at him over her glasses. 'Fortunately Leah has no need for money, unlike Mickey. I don't suppose you know of a wealthy man for her to marry?' she asked, much to Mickey's horror.

'Sophie!' she protested, knowing it was the older woman's idea of a joke, but knowing too that Ryan was not the man to appreciate it any more than she did. However, just the mere fact of her having said it meant Sophie was covering something up. 'I don't need a husband!'

'But you do need the money, dear.'

Mickey took one look at Ryan's grim expression and could have screamed. 'We weren't talking about me, Sophie. How could you let Leah go off? What about her studies?'

The older woman tutted. 'There will be time for them, Mickey. Where's your heart, child? Leah loves this young man, and right now she wants to acknowledge her commitment to him. You're her sister; surely you must understand that.'

But I don't, she wanted to shout. How could Leah do this? How could she throw away everything? How could Sophie allow it? Mickey had learnt a great deal about Leah's grandmother's rather eccentric views, and had come to accept it as normal—for her. Yet she had never expected her sister would act so recklessly.

However, there was nothing she could say, because clearly the other woman saw nothing to worry about. She sighed. Sophie, for all her worldliness, seemed sublimely unconcerned by all the pitfalls lying in wait for the unwary. Because she liked him, it would never occur to her that this man she saw as estimable might be far from that ideal. Which explained why she was acting the way she was. She had probably even expected such a visitation, and had promised to help! Sophie positively thrived on romantic intrigue.

Mickey knew from past experience that there was little point in trying to pierce Sophie's dippy persona with a frontal attack. Once in place, she could keep it up indefinitely, especially when the person for whose benefit it was being put on was in the room. There was to be no help in that direction, unless she could get Sophie alone, and that meant ditching Ryan Douglas. Right now, she didn't know how that was to be done.

'Did they say where they were going?' she asked tonelessly, trying to salvage something.

'The islands,' Sophie vouchsafed with a smile, unconcerned by just how vague a direction that was.

For the first time ever, Mickey felt her palms itch, and she eyed the other woman in exasperation. 'Which islands? The Queen Charlottes?'

Sophie shrugged, eyes limpid and innocent. 'They didn't say, and I didn't ask,' she replied, and Mickey had to stifle a gasp hastily when for a moment their eyes clashed and Sophie's were as clear as crystal and openly challenging.

'How long have they been gone?' Ryan asked with studied politeness, and, although Mickey could feel the tension in him, she had to marvel at his self-control.

The older woman removed her pince-nez and polished them vigorously. 'Two...three weeks.'

'And they haven't contacted you in all that time?' Ryan challenged disbelievingly.

'It didn't seem so long. When you get old, you don't count the time.'

If Mickey hadn't already known it, that alone would have told her that Sophie knew a great deal more than she was saying. She might disdain telephones, but she was a keen radio ham. Leah spoke to her grandmother every day without fail, and Sophie was probably waiting for a call right now! Unfortunately, if she was determined to stay close-mouthed, even a can opener wouldn't prise her open.

Ryan took the statement stoically, rising to his feet agilely. A poker-faced Mickey followed suit. 'My grandmother used to say much the same thing, but that was because she didn't want to be held to account for her sins.'

Sophie was not a whit put out, and fairly bounced to her feet. 'Young man, I'm too old to worry about sin!'

He eyed her steadily for a long time, then said softly, 'Perhaps so, but I'll assume you have a conscience. So if by some...miracle...your granddaughter does get in touch, have her tell Peter he's needed at home. Now I'm sure you'll forgive us for having to rush off,' he added with heavy irony.

'You'll come again when Leah and Peter return?'

'Oh, I think you can safely bet money on that, Sophie,' Ryan drawled with grim amusement, shaking her hand and heading for the door.

Mickey was once more enfolded in a warm embrace.

'That's one angry man, Mickey.'

'Perhaps he wouldn't have been so angry if you'd told him everything,' Mickey challenged, looking the older woman straight in the eye.

Sophie laughed. 'Dear child, what can you mean?'

Exasperated, Mickey sighed. 'You're sending me on a wild-goose chase, and I don't appreciate it.'

'Then you should. There's colour in your cheeks and a sparkle in your eye, Mickey. Ask yourself who put them there. Now run along. He's not the sort I'd want to keep waiting, although you seem to be blooming on it!' Sophie declared softly, and Mickey sent her a startled look.

'You haven't heard the last of it. I'll be back, on my own, and I'll expect answers!' she declared, before going to join the man standing impatiently on the porch.

Ryan didn't utter a word until they were once more in the jeep and on their way back to the city. 'She's quite a character.'

She wondered if he realised just how much of a character Sophie was, and found out in the next second.

'Getting the facts out of her is like trying to wade through treacle! Those two don't need an army when they've got Sophie Trenchard on their side!'

His perception brought a reluctant smile to her lips. 'One of a kind,' she acknowledged wryly, and he laughed, so that it seemed for a moment they were in accord. Mickey found it strangely unsettling.

'One is quite sufficient. Hell, they could be anywhere, and the only one who knows is pretending she lives in Cloud-cuckoo-land!' he growled, thumping his fist on the steering-wheel. 'Not that you seem to be surprised, Hanlon. Were you banking on her running interference for you? Are you still going to insist you knew nothing about it?'

That brief moment of empathy vanished. 'If I had, we wouldn't be sitting here now! I don't know how your sainted nephew managed to seduce my sister, but I'm going to put a stop to it. Damn him; Leah had everything going for her until he came along!' Mickey cried wrathfully.

Beside her, Ryan laughed grimly. 'Well, they say it's an ill wind that doesn't blow somebody something good. Look on the bright side, Hanlon. I'm going after them, and you're going to take me. So it looks as if you're going to get paid after all.'

CHAPTER THREE

'MORNING, Sid,' Mickey mumbled as she walked into the hangar next morning, smothering a yawn behind her hand.

The grizzled mechanic sent her a grin. 'Hiya, Mickey. Up early, ain't ye?'

A lack of sleep had done nothing to sweeten her mood, nor the dreadful meal she had had with Ryan Douglas after they had returned to his hotel last night. Not that the meal had been bad, just the company. It was as well she had scarcely eaten anything or she would have suffered from indigestion as well as a sleepless night.

'Mr "God Almighty" Douglas insists on catching the light!' she grunted irritably, keeping up a fiction which Ryan had insisted on. To all intents and purposes, they would be out taking photographs. For once she had not argued. She didn't want anyone to know what they would really be doing either. Publicity of the kind this search would produce, if the story ever got out, was the very last thing either of them needed.

Shaggy eyebrows rose at hearing the unaccustomed grumble. 'Sounds a reasonable request to me, Mickey,' Sid remonstrated, with the ease of long acquaintance, and she sighed heavily.

'It is, but he isn't,' she snapped, unwilling to concede more than she had to. Over a dinner which she had barely touched, Ryan had reiterated his intentions in no uncertain terms, and, considering they had the same aim, although admittedly differing viewpoints, there hadn't been anything she could reasonably take exception to. Except his persistence in still seeing Leah as a girl with

42

her eye on the main chance, a charge she had countered
by declaring his odious nephew had taken advantage of
Leah's sweet nature.

Her fleeting sympathy towards Peter Douglas had
vanished with the knowledge that he had induced her
sister to run off with him, abandoning a bright future.
She couldn't believe that Leah really loved him. What
did she know about love? She had lived a rather shel-
tered existence. As far as Mickey knew, she hadn't even
had a real boyfriend. No, she had been seduced into
thinking she was in love by a handsome face and a
blinding charm! She couldn't know that love to such
men was just an illusion, just a word glossing over needs
of a far earthier nature.

What Mickey was so dreadfully afraid of was that Leah
would find out too late. She didn't want her to be hurt
and disillusioned the way she herself had been. God, she
would do anything to protect Leah from that. She'd get
her away from the clutches of that playboy if it was the
last thing she did!

Which perversely gave her something in common with
Ryan after all. Neither wanted this match, and they were
determined to put a stop to it. But first of all they had
to find the elusive runaways.

Sid, meanwhile, waved a piece of oily rag in her direction. 'Ain't you never heard you catch more flies with
molasses, Mickey?' he observed, and she came out of
her reverie with a start.

'If you think I'm going to stroke his male ego just to
keep him sweet, you're on the wrong track. I'm sorry,
Sid, but I just can't stand the man.'

'Ain't that the truth,' he drawled, and cocked his
thumb over his shoulder. 'You gonna take her for a test
run?'

Mickey looked from the float plane to her watch. Time
was getting on, and already the sun was rising higher.
'There won't be time; I'll have to check her as we go.

Give Amelia her maximum fuel load, please, Sid. I'll do my checks as soon as I've found my charts.'

Sid tipped a finger in acknowledgement, and Mickey hurried into the office, but not before his half-muttered comment reached her ears. 'Artistic temperament they call it, girl. You gotta learn how to handle it.'

Mickey grimaced as she closed the door and leant back against it. She knew all about artistic temperament, and had spent the greater portion of her life pacifying it.

As a tiny child, Mickey's earliest memories of her mother were of being kissed goodnight by a glittering princess, or of playing with her dolls on the bathroom floor while this beautiful angel bathed in water that emitted intoxicating scents. Of course, she hadn't realised then that her mother was Tanita Amory, the Hollywood actress. She had been some god-like creature who had welcomed a little girl into her glowing world.

She had no memories of her real father, knowing only that he had been Michael Hanlon, a Canadian pilot. She had known little more about the succession of men who became her stepfathers for one or two years as she grew up. What she had learned was that her mother was so wrapped up in these men that she had very little time for her daughter. Tanita had lavished love on her by giving her all the things money could buy, but not by giving of herself.

By the time Mickey entered her teenage years, the marriages had given way to a procession of lovers. There were always new men around. Wherever they went, Tanita had flirted outrageously. Although Mickey loved her mother, she had hated her free and easy lifestyle. Tanita positively basked in the Press stories about her latest lover or husband, even as her daughter grew to hate it.

Mickey's emerging sexuality had taken place under a barrage of flashlights. Privacy was something only other people had. When she'd proved to be every bit as much of a beauty as her parent, speculation had grown. She'd become as much a target for gossip as her mother. No aspect of her life had been sacred, and when the opposite sex began to take an interest in her the papers had a field-day. Was she, they wondered, the same as her mother?

Mickey herself would have issued a firm no, until she'd met Jean-Luc Renauld. He had come into her life at an unhappy time. She had been nineteen, and just out of finishing school. She had wanted to go to university, but Tanita had flown into a rage, accusing her of being disloyal, of not loving her. Why else would she want to go away when she knew her mother needed her? Blackmail it might have been, but Mickey's sense of loyalty had made it impossible for her to argue. So she had given up all thought of studying her beloved history, of perhaps making a career for herself in the field of archaeology. Instead she had stayed in the South of France, and had met the man who was to alter her life completely.

He'd been bronzed and golden, a power-boat racer, and for the first time in her life Mickey had felt herself attracted to a man. When he had shown an interest in her, she had fallen head over heels in love with him. He had aroused a passion in her which had bedazzled her. When he had said they must be discreet, that they must meet in secret, she had ignored the knocking of her conscience which tried to tell her this was not quite right. She was in love, totally besotted, and their affair was passionate and flamboyant. Making love with Jean-Luc had been an exhilarating experience. Her senses, let loose, were in total control.

Then one day she had found her picture splashed across the front of the newspapers, the whole affair made public as she was cited in a divorce petition. Shock had broken the spell she had been under, and she knew she should have guessed Jean-Luc was married, for all the signs had been there. She had ignored them because she hadn't wanted to give him up, and she still didn't. She had gone to him, telling him she loved him and would face any scandal if it meant they could be together.

Jean-Luc's reply had instituted the most traumatic experience of her life. The man she'd thought loved her had laughed and called her a fool. A sexy fool, but still a fool. He had taken what she had offered, but he wasn't about to give up his wife for a nymphet, however exciting and inventive she was. He had gone back to his wife in the hope of stopping the divorce.

That was when Mickey had finally realised it hadn't been love at all, but lust. She had met a man and wanted him so much that nothing had mattered. She had been no better than her mother, had, in fact, inherited the very same genes. It had been a terrible thing to realise, but she had made herself face it. More than that, she knew she had a choice. If she stayed, then she feared this greedy thing inside her would lead her on from one affair to the next. But if she left... If she took herself away, plunged herself into work, she could get control of herself.

And that was what she had done. Through many tearful scenes with her mother she'd insisted that she wanted to go and find her father. Reluctantly Tanita had agreed to send someone to discover where he was, and as soon as Mickey had heard that news herself she had packed her bags and left.

Michael Hanlon had been surprised but delighted to see her. He had welcomed her into his family and his life, and Mickey hadn't looked back. Until yesterday, when Ryan Douglas had walked into her life and re-awakened that devil inside her, threatening the whole fabric of her existence.

He was in another league. He had an aura, a presence which was almost tactile, instantly alluring to the females of the species, which the tabloids, with their insatiable lust for gossip, were only too happy to reveal. It was very rare indeed for Ryan to be snapped with the same beauty more than once. For twice, the woman had to be exceptional. It was a debatable point which of his reputations was greater—that of his work as a photographer *par excellence*, or as a lover. Also *par excellence*?

The whimsical thought caught her on a vulnerable spot. She didn't want to think of Ryan as a lover. It conjured up wild visions in her mind that should have been shocking, but were, dismayingly, very far from that. Such thinking was dangerous. Besides, any woman who was crazy enough to get involved with a man like Ryan Douglas could expect to carry out that affair as if she were living in a goldfish bowl! And that was quite enough to make Mickey see reason. Her early life had been lived in a blaze of publicity, and, having escaped, she had no wish to be plunged into that particular maelstrom ever again.

The unpleasant memories which floated to the surface of her consciousness made her shiver in distaste, and, hastily crossing to her desk, she turned her thoughts to her present problems with qualified relief.

She wanted everything to be in order before her nemesis arrived. She should really have done all this groundwork last night, but she'd been too tired. If she'd known she wouldn't sleep, she would have come and done it anyway. Finding the chart, she plotted a course with the ease and speed of long practice, and was still leaning over the desk, filling out a route plan to give to Sid for safety purposes, when a flash of blinding light brought her upright in a hurry.

A fierce wave of anger tore through Mickey like a tempest as she found Ryan lounging in the doorway, hands lazily holding a camera which was looped about his neck. He looked completely at ease, his lean frame clothed in denim jeans and shirt and a navy quilted body warmer. Leather boots on his feet and that hat completed what was a damned sexy outfit—and he knew it.

What was worse, he caught the momentary flash of rec-ognition in her eyes, and it was the tiny knowing smile hovering on his mouth which made her control snap. That tiny betrayal was wormwood to her soul, and her anger sought a target on which to vent itself.

Damn it, he was just like all the rest! She had fought hard for her privacy, and now this man came along and invaded it without asking; invaded it with a devastating brand of vibrant male sexuality! He only had to enter the room and she felt embattled! Without knowing it, he lit the blue touch-paper of her pyrotechnic emotions, but, incapable of retreating any further, she was driven to advance.

'How dare you?' she cried as she crossed the floor in angry strides, hand reaching for the offending machine. 'Give me the film!'

Those damnable eyebrows rose, as with one hand he held his camera out of reach above his head, and used the other to keep her at bay. 'Take it easy, Hanlon. Don't you think you're over-reacting? It was just a snap.'

The sensible thing to have done at that point was to backpedal, but she was beyond that. All she knew was that it was galling how he could thwart her with just one hand, adding to her rage. 'It was an invasion of privacy, and I demand that you hand over the film this minute.'

He laughed grimly. 'You can demand all you like, but you're just wasting your breath. Besides, what's so wrong with me taking your picture? It's hardly a crime.'

This was a subject upon which Mickey, with the memory of her experiences forever alive in her mind, was hardly rational. Her lip curled. 'Not to you, perhaps, but to me it's stealing part of my life. I didn't give you permission, but that's never bothered your sort, has it? You take your grubby pictures and splash them round the world, and call it the people's right to know!' The words tumbled from her lips in a torrent, and it was only as the vitriolic flow slowed that she realised the error of her reaction—that anger had made her indiscreet. But even as her teeth ground shut, she knew it was too late to retract anything.

The irritating anger and mockery in his blue eyes had changed to a look of intrigue. 'Curiouser and curiouser. That sounds like the voice of experience speaking. Which naturally begs the question, who are you, Hanlon?'

Like a hermit crab, she closed in on herself for protection, and her face froze as she stiffened defensively. 'A woman of no importance, I assure you.'

'Hard to believe of someone who's had the kind of brush with the Press you've just described,' Ryan argued, making her wish, not for the first time, that she had never met the wretched man. She had disliked other men, yet managed to deal with them civilly, but he just made her temper explode.

Which was why it was certainly not the time to recall what Sophie had said last night—that there was a colour and sparkle to her which had been missing until Ryan appeared!

It was enough to fill her veins with ice, and consequently her laugh had a frosty edge to it. 'Believe me, I'm nobody, and delighted to be so. Which is why I don't like having my picture taken. May I have it, please?' Hard though it was to be polite, she knew it was her only chance of success, and a very slim one at that.

Ryan surveyed her tense face through narrowed eyes. 'That's a whole film you want me to waste, and they don't come cheap. What do I get in return?'

There was a certain quality in the timbre of his voice which sent a shiver up the length of her spine. 'My thanks,' she retorted, dismayed to find her words came out huskily.

Something flickered into life in the depths of his eyes. 'That's small change, Hanlon,' he dismissed instantly, lowering the camera and eyeing both her and it con-

sideringly. 'Tell you what I'll do: I'll give you the film
in exchange for. . . a kiss.'

Mickey's eyes widened with shock, not so much horrified by the suggestion, though that was bad enough,
as the fact that her lips had tingled as if the kiss had
already taken place! She quickly stepped away from him,
crossing her arms defensively. 'I'd sooner kiss a snake!'

The mockery made a swift return to his eyes. 'Sweetheart, I'd rather kiss a real woman, but beggars can't
be choosers. You want the film, and those are my terms.
Take it or leave it.'

The swine! She sent him a withering look. 'Thanks,
but I'll leave it. I'm not in the habit of bartering sexual
favours!' she refused acidly, desperate to hide the fact
that for that one fleeting, crazy moment her traitorous
thoughts had her wondering just what it would be like
to be kissed by him. To have that sensual mouth moving
on hers, pressing her to open to him, invading her. . .
With a shiver she clamped down ruthlessly on thoughts
which could set her on a course she was determined never
to travel again.

Oblivious to her inner struggle, Ryan shrugged. 'Suit
yourself, but it's an open-ended offer. Any time you feel
like taking it up, just tell me,' he went on, then, before
she could stop him, quickly raised the camera and
snapped off another shot. 'But it's only fair to warn you
that the interest will keep rising all the time. It's two
shots now, so that's two kisses, if you want them back.'

Mickey ground her teeth in angry impotence. She
longed to respond, but he was just waiting for that, and
she refused to give him the satisfaction. What more proof
did she need that he was as lacking in moral integrity as
all the others? Yet, having decided that, perversely she
felt disappointment, as if he had let not just her down,
but himself, and that was crazy thinking. She disliked
the man, so what did it matter if she didn't think well
of him?

Of course it didn't matter, she told herself firmly as she turned back to the desk and reached for her charts. Facing him again, her demeanour was one of brisk efficiency. 'Shall we get on? After all, we're wasting valuable time.'

Amused by the change, he stood back pointedly to let her pass through the door. 'Lead the way, Hanlon. You're in charge.'

It was a relief to get out of the small room and breathe more freely. 'I'm glad you realise it,' she sent back caustically over her shoulder.

'In all things aeronautical, that is. There can be only one leader in any expedition, and I'm it. When it comes to finding the runaways, what I say goes.'

If they were laying down rules, then she was only too happy to oblige, and make some of her own. 'If you want me to agree to take your orders, then you'll have to keep your nose out of my private life.'

'Do you actually have a private life? I had the idea you only love your aeroplane,' came the ironic rejoinder.

Though she knew it wasn't wise to bring herself down to his level, it was impossible to resist. 'They respond to the loving care bestowed on them, which is more than can be said for the average male!'

'Perhaps your problem is you've only ever known average males,' Ryan countered smoothly, his long stride easily bringing him into step beside her.

It was like coming into contact with a force field, one which drew you in rather than held you back, and instantly Mickey wanted to move away from him. It was a childishly defensive act, and she resisted it, but she could hardly ignore the total awareness of him she was experiencing every time he came within a few feet of her. It made her skin prickle, sending a tingle throughout her system that she just couldn't prevent. She didn't want to feel it, but it seemed beyond her control.

A wave of self-disgust churned her stomach. She had tried so hard to stifle these urges within her, to control them and not let them ruin her life as they had before. She didn't want to be dragged down into that pit again where her every action was guided by her passions. She would fight her genes with every ounce of strength inside her! But she had to be careful not to give off signals. She didn't want to make any move that would make this highly intuitive man aware of just what she was feeling. If he should guess that she was dangerously vulnerable to him in the most basic way, her pride could be crushed forever.

She had never been so glad that she hadn't allowed herself to be affected by his jeering and so was wearing her usual clothes. The loose-fitting plaid shirt hid the fact that her breasts had responded to his closeness, her nipples hardening into points which brushed teasingly against the material. She might feel exposed, but she wasn't, and that gave her the necessary spirit to stay put and say, 'I don't have a problem.'

He sent her another of those all-encompassing sideways glances. 'You think it's natural to cut men out of your life, and attempt to act like one yourself?'

Sickened by his prurient curiosity, Mickey came to a halt beside her float plane and turned to Ryan with her chest heaving in righteous indignation. 'I don't cut men out, or hadn't you noticed I work with one?' She inclined her head to where Sid was finishing tanking up the small craft.

Ryan didn't allow himself to be diverted. 'He's a good man, but old enough to be your grandfather. We're talking about younger men.'

Her raised hand cut him off. '*We* aren't talking about them at all; you are. And as it's a subject I find tedious in the extreme, why don't we change it?' It wasn't so much a suggestion as an order, and he ignored it like all the others. Resting a hand against the metal bodywork of the float plane, he successfully stopped her from climbing inside while he studied her with unfeigned curiosity.

'What are you so afraid of? You wouldn't be a virgin by any chance, would you, Hanlon?'

The question, coming out of a clear blue sky the way it did, floored her. Mickey's cheeks first went white then red as she floundered around for an answer that wouldn't choke her. 'That is none of your damn business!' She couldn't believe how these conversations kept happening. Whatever they started talking about, somehow the subject of her personal life always came up.

Amusement danced in his eyes. 'Hmm, intriguingly non-committal. At least you've got that feminine art off to a T. There's hope for you yet.'

Dear God, but he was infuriating! She drew herself up to her full height. '*Mr* Douglas...' His name was as far as she got, for with an agile movement he levered himself up into the aircraft, bending to observe her standing looking helplessly up at him.

'You'd better get a move on, Hanlon; the light's changing fast, and we wouldn't want anyone to think the light isn't important, even if we know better,' he taunted before he disappeared completely, leaving her choking on her fury.

Unsettled, she found she had to do all the outside checks twice because she'd been too angry to register what she was seeing the first time. Yet the sheer act of following the set routine had the effect of calming her down, so that by the time she joined him inside she was once more fully in control. It was a return to sanity, having to keep her mind on the job in hand, and she swiftly completed the pre-flight checks. Putting on the headphones sealed her into a world of her own.

'Come on, Amelia, don't let me down now,' she urged under her breath, because the old girl had become rather temperamental about starting lately. This time, though, there was no hesitation, and in less than five minutes they were airborne.

Automatically she relaxed, as she was once more in her element. The thrill of flying was like nothing she had ever experienced. The freedom was ultimate, just her skill against the elements. She circled the harbour once, then headed the float plane on her chosen course. Almost without knowing it, she began to hum a jaunty tune as she kept an alert look around them, and gradually the tense line of her lips softened into a smile of pure pleasure.

'You've a nice smile, when you bother to use it.'

Ryan's voice spoke the observation directly into her ear, making her jump and turn her head sharply. She found he had put on his own headset and was using it to talk to her. The smile changed to a scowl as she discovered she wasn't safe from him anywhere.

'What's the matter? Don't you like compliments?'

She met the challenging glint in his eye for a second before looking away. They were heading for the Inside Passage. Over to the west lay the misty shape of the Queen Charlotte Islands. She had always found them endlessly fascinating, but today they failed to charm, and she knew why.

'It's not compliments I don't like, it's you!' And the way the sound of his voice had made her stomach clench.

His laughter sounded so intimately close that she couldn't stop a sensual shiver running through her. 'Honest to the point of bluntness! Haven't you heard you catch more flies with honey?' he taunted, unwittingly using virtually the same phrase as Sid had, much to her annoyance.

'I'm not interested in catching flies,' Mickey retorted tersely, knowing she meant it, but appalled that her body seemed bent on ignoring the dictates of her brain.

He made a sound, somewhere between a grunt and a smothered laugh. 'Why Amelia?' he queried. 'Is she in the habit of letting you down?'

Despite his presence, her face softened, and for a moment she forgot to be defensive. 'It was my father's idea, after Amelia Earhart, the aviatrix. And no, for her age, Amelia's remarkably well behaved,' Mickey responded, mentally crossing her fingers that nothing should happen to gainsay her.

Ryan turned a little sideways to keep her profile in view. 'Like her pilot. It would nearly kill you to misbehave, wouldn't it, Hanlon?'

She stiffened instantly, as a sudden replay of events she longed to forget passed across her mind's eye. 'There's nothing to be gained by it,' she said shortly, wishing the subject closed, but knowing, trapped as she was, there was nothing she could do if he chose to go on. Which, naturally, he did.

'Admit it—wouldn't you like to do just one thing that was a little wicked?' Ryan taunted, and she could feel his eyes probing her resolutely turned profile.

Mickey bit back a too revealing retort, and forced herself to laugh. 'I've been toying with murder for the last twenty-four hours. Is that what you mean?' she enquired with mock-sweetness.

Though she couldn't see it, his lips curved into a rueful smile. 'Not exactly, but it does remind me that you have a lethal weapon at your disposal,' he rejoined drily.

Now that did make her laugh, the sound gurgling out of her. For once she actually felt she had the better of him. 'Scared, Ryan? Perhaps you should be more careful not to provoke me.'

'I reassure myself with the knowledge that you can't get rid of me without doing the same to yourself. By the by, this might be the right time to tell you I'm a qualified pilot myself. So if you were planning on looping the loop in the hopes of making me part with my breakfast, you're going to be disappointed,' Ryan added, taking his attention away from her to glance out of the side-window.

Mickey just managed to stop her jaw from dropping. Damn him. He was so sharp that one of these days he was going to cut himself! 'I wouldn't stoop to anything so childish,' she lied swiftly, saying farewell to all the little turbulent manoeuvres she had planned on making.

'Oh, I believe you, Hanlon. It's not the sort of thing a well brought-up young lady would do,' he mocked back, and there was only one safe way to deal with the statement—by ignoring it.

'If you can fly, what do you need me for?' She homed in on what seemed to her to be a vital question.

'Because while you're with me, you can't be telling your sister I'm on her trail, and so give her a chance to spirit Peter away,' Ryan informed her shortly.

Scorn filled the eyes she turned on him. 'You're crazy if you think I'd be likely to help them! I want to find them too, and stop Leah from making a mess of her life! If you think I'd let your precious nephew get his filthy hands on her, you're mistaken!' Mickey put him straight vehemently.

The bluntness was neither appreciated nor believed. 'There's nothing wrong with Peter, except a tendency to believe anything a pretty face tells him. No doubt your sister has spun a web of lies and now he's well and truly caught up in them. She wouldn't be the first girl who found making her way through university a hard slog, and looked around for the first source of easy money she could come by.'

By this time Mickey was positively fuming, a semi-permanent state of affairs with this man around. 'For the last time, Leah doesn't need money! I'd be more interested in knowing what this candidate for canonisation was doing swanning about the islands when summer is definitely over. Looking for someone gullible

enough to fall for his polished lies and charm, no doubt!'
she accused scornfully.

She didn't need to see his flaring nostrils to know Ryan
was angry too. His anger was filling the tiny cockpit with
nerve-tingling energy. 'Stop trying to make him into some
sort of Bluebeard. Peter had been on a short sabbatical
before taking up an internship. It was when he didn't
turn up at the family home on the day he was expected
that my brother and sister-in-law began to worry. You
can imagine their shock when that letter arrived.'

Mickey's surprise at realising the runaways had a vocation in common disarmed her belief that Peter was a
playboy. However, she wasn't giving up so easily. 'Do
you always play nursemaid to your nephew? Why aren't
his parents here instead?'

'Because...' he began angrily, then stopped himself,
jaw flexing, before carrying on. 'Because my brother is
a diplomat, and can't take off at a moment's notice, and
my sister-in-law has a new baby to care for. She had a
rough time, being rather older than most expectant
mothers, and Peter has looked after his brothers and
sisters for the last few months.'

Mickey knew that wasn't what he had been going to
say at all, and she resented the fact that he wouldn't tell
her the truth. Automatically she refused to be impressed. 'That doesn't make him a saint,' she rallied.

'Nor your sister,' Ryan rejoined swiftly.

Mickey closed her lips on another retort which would
have only sent them round the same course again. 'You
know, I'm beginning to really dislike you.'

He laughed drily. 'Believe me, it's mutual.'

There was no good reason why such a statement from
a complete stranger should give her any pain, but the
fact remained that it did. Something sharp entered her
heart, and it took a surprising amount of effort not to
let it show on her face. The implications of her reactions
were ones she didn't dare think about.

It was a relief to bring her concentration back to their task. 'We'll be into the Passage in a few minutes. Are you going to tell me now why you insisted we come this way?'

'Because Peter was sailing his own yacht. His family have had postcards from all his stopping-off points. The last was from Victoria, but there have been none since. He had to come north to get here, so it's my guess that south is the way they'll go.'

Mickey couldn't disagree with the logic of that, although there was an alternative, albeit a doubtful one. 'Did it occur to you that he might have thought of that and decided to keep heading north up to Skagway?'

Ryan rubbed a hand rather tiredly around his neck, as if the choice he had made had not been without effort. 'He could have, but I came to the conclusion that I can't be everywhere at once, and I had to start somewhere. So take her down, Hanlon, and let's get this over with as quickly and as painlessly as possible.'

Although she agreed with the sentiment, Mickey balked at his habit of throwing his weight around. 'I wish to goodness you'd stop ordering me around! I do know how to conduct a search. Unfortunately it's something we have to do rather too often up here.'

'You're part of a search and rescue team?'

'There's no need to sound so surprised. Most folks up here help one way or another. We often have to rely on ourselves when winter closes in,' she revealed as she eased the stick forward and they began to lose height. 'It's something most city dwellers don't think of.'

'Hmm, but you can't really blame them; they've been conditioned to expect their creature comforts,' Ryan agreed.

She spared him a frowning glance. 'You said that as if you exclude yourself.'

His smile was wry. 'That's because my home is out in the hills. I may not have to use a plane to do it, but we have to rescue the foolhardy, too.'

It irked her no end to discover there was something else to admire about him. Yet her dislike wouldn't allow her to denigrate him. 'Mountain rescue? You have hidden talents.'

'Peeved, Hanlon?' he chided in amusement, and she grimaced.

'I admire what you do too much to be peeved, but that doesn't make us friends either,' she replied quellingly.

'Then it's just as well I never thought it would,' Ryan confessed, and gave his attention to the scenery unfolding beneath them. 'Hell, this is worse than a maze.'

Mickey silently agreed. The task ahead of them was monumental. She only hoped they would find the runaways today, because spending too much time in this man's company would be downright dangerous.

CHAPTER FOUR

MICKEY and Ryan diligently searched every inlet and island they passed over as they headed south, until Mickey's neck was aching from being held for so long at an unnatural angle. At any other time she would have marvelled anew at the spectacular landscape. There was an almost prehistoric look to the sloping, tree-covered hills and hump-backed islands of the Inside Passage. But today all it served to remind her of was the astronomical task ahead of them, and that the odds of meeting with success were infinitesimal. Summer might be over, but there was still plenty of traffic using the sparkling waters.

However, as they flew close to Hartley Bay, Mickey suddenly had a brainwave. She had known last night that she needed to speak to Sophie alone, but the means of doing so hadn't been apparent. Now, by a stroke of pure luck, she remembered this was the day for her eccentric relative to visit a friend in Kemano, and that was little more than a hop, skip and jump away by air! The problem was, as ever, Ryan Douglas. She'd have to ditch him, or she'd never get the chance to be alone.

Just then her stomach growled, reminding her that it was lunchtime. In an instant she had the inkling of a plan. They were pretty close to a favourite spot of hers. If she was to put down there, she might just be able to make some excuse to get back to Amelia without him, and fly off and see Sophie. Of course, he wouldn't just up and let her go; she'd have to lull him, be nice to him. She could surely do that for as long as it took, and face the inevitable consequences of stranding him later.

'You might as well put her down somewhere, Hanlon, and we'll have some lunch. We could both do with a break,' Ryan suggested right out of the blue, making Mickey jump guiltily.

Looking at him, she could have kicked herself. Here he was, falling right into her plans, and now she remembered she'd forgotten all about packing lunch! 'I forget to bring any food,' she confessed morosely, sick with disappointment.

'It's fortunate, then, that I had the hotel provide enough for two. Sid put the hamper in the back,' he informed her. 'Choose a nice spot, and we can have a picnic.'

Considering she had been about to suggest virtually the same thing, the way Mickey's nerves leapt in response to the idea was a blow. It should have meant nothing, yet suddenly sharing a picnic conjured up an intimate scene quite different from merely having lunch. Dormant senses tingled into wakefulness. She hated the way she seemed to have no control over her body. Even knowing he put the suggestion that way to get a rise out of her didn't lessen the response. And though she longed to refuse, she knew she couldn't, or she'd lose her chance to get away.

Hoist by her own petard, she sent him a tense smile. 'There's a place along from here which will suit us perfectly,' she agreed shortly, banking Amelia to the right.

Within minutes she brought the float plane down, and taxied in to a tiny cove. To their left a rocky promontory was dotted with firs, but just round to their right, and hidden from view, she knew a large boulder formed the ideal viewpoint.

'We can sit on there and watch the world go by while we eat,' Mickey explained, suddenly realising she had never actually brought anyone here before. In fact there were other places she could have picked, and kept this one private. So why, then, had she automatically chosen it for Ryan to see, and why was her heart tripping along at a faster rate? There was a bitter taste in her mouth. What was it her subconscious was trying to tell her, for heaven's sake?

Unnoticed, Ryan watched emotions varying from dismay to confusion flicker across her face. 'This is hardly Main Street, USA.'

Mickey blinked at him, feeling a surprisingly keen sense of disappointment. It did nothing for her confidence to realise that she had actually wanted him to like the site, and that wasn't just ridiculous, it was dangerous. Having been about to get up, she hastily sat back down again, reaching for the starter. 'I was referring to the wildlife. I thought, judging by the pictures you take, that you might be interested. I was wrong, so we'll go somewhere else,' she said shortly, not knowing exactly why she felt the way she did, but wishing she didn't feel it anyway.

With a fluid movement, Ryan reached out and prevented her from firing the engine, drawing her mutinous green gaze as he did so. 'This will be perfect, and I apologise for making that fatuous remark. You took me by surprise. I didn't imagine this was your sort of thing.'

Trying not to reveal how the warmth of his touch had taken her breath away, she raised her brows in disdain. 'Would I live here if it wasn't?'

His smile became sardonic. 'That depends on your reasons for being here. However, I'm prepared to give you the benefit of the doubt for the sake of my stomach. OK, Hanlon, you lead the way and I'll bring the food.'

Gnashing her teeth, Mickey glared at him. 'Don't do me any favours! You might think I'm a joke, but frankly I don't give a damn!' she snapped, jerking away from him to stand up.

He laughed. 'You remind me of a kitten who doesn't know whether to spit or purr. Well, I've found food generally puts animals and people in a better humour, so the best thing I can do right now is feed you!' he declared as he rose and followed her out.

Mickey experienced an overwhelming urge to thrust his food down his mocking throat, but remembered just in time that she was supposed to be lulling, not antagonising him. She nearly choked on her spleen, though, and was glad she had her back to him so he couldn't see her scowl. Having tied up the plane, she led the way round and up on to the top of the rock, going right over to the edge before she sat down. Ryan joined her, opening the hamper and laying out packets of sandwiches, some fruit and a Thermos of coffee.

After eating in silence for a while, Mickey knew she would have to say something before it got too late to act. Sighing, she sent him a smile she had learned at her expensive finishing school, hoping he wouldn't see how plastic it was. 'You were right about the food. I'm sorry I was so grouchy. It's been a pretty awful twenty-four hours.'

For a moment he said nothing, merely eyed her over the top of his mug of coffee, then he smiled. 'You're forgiven.'

His condescension was a goad she forced herself to ignore. If only it was as easy to ignore the craving the sensual curve of his lips unleashed inside her. 'Thank you.'

Blue eyes danced, or it could have been sunlight. 'What kinds of wildlife do you get around here?' Ryan asked, abandoning his food in favour of focusing his camera on the panorama before them.

She latched on to the safe topic gratefully. 'Apart from the native birds and animals, along the coast you can see sealions, whales and dolphins. Once I thought I saw a bald eagle, but it was just a speck really, so far in the distance.' Looking away, she sighed reminiscently. 'It made me feel good, though, to think I might have seen one.'

Having snapped off several shots, Ryan lowered his camera, stretching himself out, tucking his hands beneath his head, and closing his eyes. 'I felt the same when I saw a condor in the Andes. I tried to capture the essence of it on film, but I don't think I was entirely successful.'

Fascinated despite herself, Mickey crossed her legs and leant forward, elbows on knees. 'I saw that one in an exhibition, and you're wrong. You showed the power and grace wonderfully. In fact, all your photographs seem to reflect hope—things as they could be, and should be.'

Ryan heaved a deep sigh. 'When you've seen too much of the dark side of life, you have to do something else to cleanse your soul.'

'You said something like that before, about war being a dirty business, but there were no war photos in the exhibition,' she probed carefully.

'I covered several of the African wars, and they weren't pretty. The trouble was, although I wanted people to see war as the monster it is, the public have been glutted with so many photographs that they all too often see them only as art and not as a visual journal of horror. So I decided to go the other way, show human dignity rather than suffering.'

'And you succeeded. With me, anyway,' Mickey responded naturally.

Ryan yawned widely. 'Sounds as if you're a fan, Hanlon,' he murmured sleepily.

Mickey held her breath, watching as he visibly relaxed before her eyes. For once the luck seemed to be on her side. He was falling asleep. 'I'm not a philistine. I admire good work when I see it,' she admitted, and waited for a caustic reply. None came, only the rhythmic rise and fall of his chest.

She waited a good five minutes before she dared stand up, and then moved very cautiously down to the ground.

The urge to take to her heels was strong, but she knew that would make too much noise. She simply hurried as quickly as she could. Amelia came into view, and Mickey laughed. Sophie, here I come.

She was just praising herself for having made good her escape when a dark figure fairly leapt from the trees ahead of her, into her path. Her scream of fright was instinctive, and had barely died away when she recognised Ryan, and her heart lurched sickeningly. Damn it, she had almost made it. She had almost escaped him!

Mickey paled as the silent cry tore the blinkers from her eyes. She hadn't been running to Sophie so much as away from him! Away from the way he made her feel. Getting to Sophie was merely a convenient excuse.

The mockery on his face taunted her. 'Going somewhere, Hanlon?'

It was hard to frame a reply through her anguish of mind. 'Y-you were asleep. I . . . th-thought I'd pack up while you slept,' she invented, before realising the stupidity of the claim. She'd left everything back on the rock, as he very well knew.

Angry blue eyes narrowed contemptuously. 'I "slept", sweetheart, because I knew that was what you wanted. I knew something was up the minute you started being friendly. In order to find out what it was, I fell in with your wishes. When you left, I followed you.' He took a step towards her, arms belligerently akimbo. 'What were you going to do—strand me here?'

A hot tide of colour flooded her cheeks, and was answer enough although she did try to say something in mitigation 'No, I——'

He cut her off. 'Yes! You were going to leave me here while you went off to meet your sister!' Ryan thundered, every angry word making her flinch. 'You're playing games with me, Hanlon, and I don't like it! I don't have time for any more, so name your price.'

She didn't even have to think about it. She would never take money from this or any man. 'No!'

Ryan's wrath was awesome. 'Not enough? Why you mercenary little...' He got a grip on himself with an effort. With a rough laugh he dragged a hand through his hair. 'Hell, Peter's brother Bobby is lying in a coma, and I'm wasting time trying to make a deal with you. There's only one way: I'll write you a blank cheque, no questions asked, if you take me to them.'

Mickey's head reeled. 'What did you say?' she choked.

There was a nasty look on his face now. 'I thought that would hit you where you live, Hanlon,' he sneered.

It took her a vital second to realise he thought she was referring to the money. She sent him a daggers look. 'Not that—about Peter's brother.'

Ryan shook his head slowly. 'Now this I don't believe. Are you trying to pretend you have a conscience? Don't expect me to believe that hearing my nephew is in a coma after an accident will make any difference.'

He might not believe it, but it did, all the same. It would make a difference to Sophie, too, when she heard. But there was little point in telling Ryan, for he had such a low opinion of her that he would never change his mind. Not that there was time to worry over that. It was imperative that she get a message to Sophie by whatever means she could, and as quickly as possible.

Without looking at him, she turned around and began making her way back to the rock. 'We'd better get moving. It won't be long before we have to turn back anyway.' She hadn't taken more than a few steps before Ryan halted her with a hand on her shoulder.

'So you don't have a better side. That's hardly news to me, but I'd like an answer to my offer,' he ordered, eyes quartering her face.

She shrugged him off, although her shoulder wore the heat of his touch like a brand. 'Let's get two things straight: I don't want your money, neither can I take you to them, because I don't know where they are!' she reiterated.

'Then why the attempt to strand me?' he countered icily, and she flared up instantly.

'Because any sane woman would want to get as far away from you as she could!' she cried in exasperation.

'Honey, no sane man would let you within a hundred miles of him if he had a choice! But I'm stuck with you, so let's go get the hamper; we've wasted enough time.'

'This is hopeless!' Mickey exclaimed several hours later, blinking eyes which felt stiff from continual raking of the view below them. 'It's like looking for a needle in a haystack! Have you any idea just how many bays and inlets there are out here, not to mention islands? And we don't even know if we're going in the right direction.'

Ryan, who had remained withdrawn and silent throughout the afternoon, except to issue curt orders which she had responded to with teeth clenched, turned to afford her one of his inimical looks. 'Do you have a better idea?'

Mickey released an irritated breath. She didn't, not until she spoke to Sophie, which left them right where they were. 'Surely your nephew must have said something to someone? He must have friends.'

Ryan smiled grimly. 'He has, but if he spoke to them they're saying nothing. What about your sister? Did you try her room-mates?'

She had done that the instant she returned to her house last night, and it had been a frustrating half-hour. 'Close as clams.'

'You have to admire their loyalty.' He sounded drily amused, which didn't please Mickey.

'No, I don't! I don't like all this sneaking around and underhandedness. Leah never did anything like it before she met your precious nephew. She was always so open about everything.' And that was one of the deepest

wounds—to know Leah had felt she must keep her romance to herself. Mickey couldn't understand it, because they had always shared confidences. Why had she
suddenly been afraid to say anything?

'Perhaps she knew what reaction she would get,' Ryan
observed, and met her shocked gaze squarely as she
swung round.

'What is that supposed to mean?' she demanded
sharply, and saw one enigmatic eyebrow lift.

'Somehow I doubt you'd be happy whoever she fell
in love with,' he said bluntly, and she gasped aloud.

'That's a nasty thing to suggest! I want Leah to be
happy, of course I do!' she protested vigorously.

The other brow rose to join its mate. 'Then why the
automatic assumption that Peter's a vile seducer? Strong
words when you don't even know the man.' As he spoke
his eyes narrowed on her pale cheeks. 'Or have I hit on
the truth here? Are you so anti-men because that was
the very thing which happened to you?'

The accuracy of that guess sent a chill through her,
and for a moment she felt as if he knew everything that
had ever happened to her. It was impossible to continue
looking at him, and she turned away, concentrating
fiercely on her controls. But it was equally impossible
not to think of what he had said. Had she done that?
Were her motives totally personal, and not geared to
Leah at all? Yet was it wrong to want to protect her
sister from the possible pitfalls of life? She was so sweet,
so trusting, a sitting duck for an experienced man of the
world.

And yet it was true she didn't know anything about
Peter Douglas. Shouldn't she wait and reserve
judgement? But what if he turned out to be anything
like his uncle? Ryan's assumptions about Leah were every
bit as bad as her own, a thought which had her raising
her chin belligerently.

'You're forgetting that you've accused Leah of being a gold-digger with just as little justification! It's obvious Peter didn't confide in you, either. Which gives you no right to crow. Instead of digging your nose into my business, why don't you come clean as to why you were kept in the dark too?'

Ryan's face reflected a scornful irony. 'Probably because not six months ago I was bailing him out of another mess he'd got himself into. It was a nasty piece of attempted blackmail, all because he'd fallen for the sob story of a druggie who had discovered his father is a wealthy diplomat. He swore he'd learnt his lesson, but now there's this. As I see it, why keep the relationship a secret if everything is above-board?'

My God! Mickey thought, appalled. What sort of man had Leah got herself involved with? She had been right the first time. The sooner she got Leah away from him, the better!

She let out a scoffing noise. 'Nice friends your nephew mixes with. If I find he's hurt Leah in any way, I'll create a stink you won't be able to raise your delicate noses above!'

The way his face closed up sent a warning shiver down her spine. 'A word to the wise, Hanlon. My only reaction to threats is to take them on, and I never lose a fight. My resources are greater than yours. Do you really want the kind of publicity I could organise?'

Mickey swallowed a tight lump of dread which had risen to block her throat at the mere mention of publicity. 'I'm not afraid of you! Besides, there's no such thing as bad publicity.' She was whistling in the dark, and feared he knew it.

He eyed her shrewdly for long, silent seconds. 'Hmm. People are apt to do a lot of digging when names like ours are involved. Are you sure you want your past raked up?' he mused.

Mickey felt her stomach churn sickeningly. She had been trying to bury her past for the last eight years. There were things she didn't want to remember—shameful things, and painful truths. To have all that splashed across the tabloids would kill her. As yet, it was no more than a threat of a possibility, but it was something she couldn't afford to ignore. Which was why she took a steadying breath.

'I did say *if* he's hurt her,' she pointed out huskily, and hated the way his eyes narrowed speculatively.

'So you're a lady with a past, Hanlon? The mind boggles at just what it was you did that you don't want revealed. Seeing the way you're dressed, I'd have to guess at robbing banks,' Ryan proposed, but the mockery in his voice told her it wasn't a serious suggestion, just another less than subtle dig at her lifestyle.

Her lips thinned. 'Very amusing,' she snapped sourly, and he laughed outright, the sound hitting her stomach and making it clench fiercely, while every nerve-end in her body seemed to jump to attention. Lord, but it wasn't fair. She had successfully battened down her awareness of him since lunch, and now with one laugh he had broken through, and she could feel her body tense at his closeness.

From the corner of her eye she could see the muscular length of his thigh outlined by his jeans. Her mouth went dry as a string of erotic pictures flashed through her mind. Of entangled limbs, and flesh moving on flesh. They so much shocked her that she paled even as her blood began to sizzle, and she hastily averted her eyes. Dear God, she must stop these crazy thoughts! She'd known the man for less than twenty-four hours. It was disgusting to be *lusting* after him, and with no encouragement whatsoever!

She had to pull herself together, she declared silently, and then was forced to of necessity when the engine spluttered before hiccuping on its way again. Mickey sat up straighter in her seat, automatically checking the fuel gauge.

Beside her, Ryan came to attention. 'What's wrong?'

Mickey frowned, answering absently, 'It's not fuel. Sid filled her up, and she's still showing plenty.' She tapped the gauge to make sure, but it remained steady. Which left only one answer. 'We've been having some trouble with the feed, but Sid thought he'd solved the problem.' Hoped he had, because he knew they couldn't afford the expense of a major repair.

'Are you going to have to put her down?' There was no alarm in his voice, just an understandable concern.

Mickey shook her head. 'No-o. She seems all right now. Perhaps it was just a bit of dirt.' Relief made her turn to him with a rueful smile. 'Sorry if that worried you. It's at times like these you remember all that space underneath you. Fortunately there's so much water, I can put Amelia down anywhere.'

There was a split second when it seemed as if Ryan hadn't heard a word she had said, but with a brief shake of his head he answered her. 'I wasn't worried. It didn't take more than five minutes in your company to realise you're a first-class pilot. And as I said ... you should smile more often, Hanlon.'

The unexpected warmth she had felt at his praise of her flying was instantly swamped by a wave of another kind of heat altogether, and this was centred a long way from her cheeks. Having already realised she was fighting a battle with herself, this was the last thing she needed. 'Don't get personal!' she ordered waspishly, words being her only means of defence.

Blue eyes ran over her in lazy speculation. 'There's something about you, Hanlon, that keeps getting under my skin.' His voice dropped an octave. 'Which makes the thought of getting "personal" much more of an enticement.'

Though she knew full well the declaration was meant to tease her into a reaction, what she felt was nothing so simple. His words reached her at one level, but his tone of voice was like a caress upon her skin. It seemed to cut through all her clothes, and everywhere it touched fires burned. She hadn't experienced anything quite like this before, but she knew the signs. Her senses were taking over, undermining the common sense which had been her prop and saviour. She had believed she had conquered them, but now she knew she had just been fooling herself.

'No come-back?' he goaded, when she had remained silent too long, and because she was so disgusted with herself she responded without thinking.

'Actions speak louder than words,' she declared brittly, and banked the craft so sharply that, unprepared, Ryan was rocked against the side and cracked his head audibly.

Not that he was angry; far from it. Rubbing his head, he gave a low laugh. 'There's a lot of suppressed emotion in you, Hanlon. One day it's going to burst free. I'd like to be there to see the man who has to deal with it.'

Mickey flattened the plane out before sending him a withering look. 'Why should a man be involved?'

Ryan eyed her curiously. 'Because it's a man who's roused the sleeping volcano,' he drawled.

Anger at the way she had left herself open for that was a flame in her stomach. 'You flatter yourself if you think it's you!'

He spread his hands. 'There's no other man around.'

'Which means you have to know my dislike is entirely for you!' she shot back.

'Ah, but dislike is better than nothing. It spices up an otherwise bland dish. I'm beginning to think I might be developing a taste for what's on the menu after all.'

Mickey didn't know whether to laugh, cry or scream, and could have easily done all three if it wouldn't have given him far too much of an advantage. 'You're too late. Everything's off. If you want to eat, you're going to have to go somewhere else!' she told him firmly, and prayed he would take the hint and shut up.

Ryan Douglas, however, was a law unto himself. She had decided that much the very second she'd set eyes on him. He proved it by ignoring her pointed 'No Trespassing' signs.

'Tch, tch, Hanlon, you're experienced enough to know that when a person has a craving for a certain kind of food no other could satisfy his appetite.'

Though every instinct she possessed was telling her he was doing it on purpose, that he wasn't really serious, and was only intent on winding her up, there was no way she could stop herself from retaliating. 'Then he'll just have to go hungry!'

He laughed under his breath. 'That doesn't make it go away; it simply makes the craving worse, while heightening the anticipation,' he told her, holding her simmering gaze. 'But if you don't watch out, it isn't food we'll be getting, but an early bath!'

The words were a shock to her system, and with a startled cry Mickey looked ahead to realise they were getting dangerously close to the water. She pulled the stick back while her heart thudded wildly in her chest. Only when they were on an even keel again did she dare spare him a glance.

'You're despicable!'

'And you understood every word I said,' he goaded softly, making her colour fluctuate.

'I'm not a child. I understand innuendo, even if I don't appreciate it!'

His eyes ran lazily up and down the length of her. 'No, you're not a child. A child wouldn't have responded the way you did. Admit it, Hanlon, you were just a tiny bit aroused, weren't you?'

Mickey spluttered to get a denial out, even as one part of her brain was admitting that what he said was true.

Her imagination had worked overtime, making a picture that had absolutely nothing to do with food. And it had stirred her as no other picture could have done. Which was why she hated him so much: for resurrecting a side of her nature which she loathed.

'Nothing you could ever say or do would arouse me to anything more than anger and dislike,' she managed to articulate frigidly. 'You enjoy playing games, but I don't like being the butt of them. We're out here for one reason only, and that's to find our respective relations. I suggest we concentrate on that and nothing else.'

She might just as well not have spoken at all.

'What are you running from, Hanlon, the past or yourself? Because if it's the latter, you'll find you never can outrun it, and the only thing you can do is come to terms with it,' Ryan advised sardonically before finally withdrawing from the battle, turning his shoulder and resuming the search.

Mickey stared ahead, green eyes stinging with suppressed tears. As she turned for home, every beat of her heart rang out the litany, I hate him. I hate him. I hate him.

As soon as they landed back at the jetty late that afternoon Mickey left Amelia in Sid's capable hands and, ignoring Ryan, who had stopped to talk to the mechanic, hurried into the boat shed and across to her office. Finding the telephone number of Sophie's friend, she fumbled with the dial and crossed her fingers that the old lady would still be there. Keeping one eye on the door, knowing that she only had a limited time, she urged someone to answer the ring.

It was Sophie herself who answered, and her dislike of the telephone was immediately apparent in her voice. 'Infernal machine! Yes? What do you want?'

Mickey's fingers tightened on the receiver. 'Sophie! Thank goodness! Don't hang up; it's Mickey. I have to talk to you,' she said urgently.

'Mickey? Dear child. Can't you come over? You know how I hate these contraptions,' Sophie complained.

'No, there isn't time. Now listen, Sophie, and don't interrupt. I know you're in contact with Leah, and you've got to get a message to her. Tell her to tell Peter that his brother has had an accident. He's in hospital, and his family want Peter to come home. Have you got that, Sophie? Do you understand? This isn't a game any more.'

The change in Sophie Trenchard was instant. 'Yes, I understand, dear. I'll pass that on when they contact me tonight. Good heavens, why couldn't the man have told us that last night?'

Mickey pulled a face. 'He doesn't trust us . . . me,' she sighed, and very nearly hit the roof when a grim voice spoke behind her.

'No, I don't, and it appears I have every cause not to. Who are you talking to, Hanlon?' Ryan declared, walking further into the room.

Mickey slammed the phone down. 'Nobody,' she denied nervously, licking lips which had suddenly gone dry.

'Do you often ring nobody?' he challenged brusquely, eyes like blue flints. 'You were speaking to Leah, weren't you? Telling her to stay away.'

Her chin rose. 'If I was speaking to Leah, I would have told her to come home!' She was tempted to tell him what she had been doing, but, knowing Ryan, she thought he would rush off to Kitimat, causing all sorts of problems. Sophie needed time, not harassment. 'If you must know, I was talking to my fiancé.'

She hadn't known she was going to say that, but realised it was the ideal solution. Besides, she had invented a mythical fiancé some time ago to head off her mother, whose letters had a tendency to go on about the lack of men in her daughter's life. It had done its job, but of late Tanita had begun to wonder why the engagement was going on so long, with no sign of a wedding. However, that had nothing to do with this. She needed to keep Ryan at a distance, and this was perfect. Unfortunately he was disinclined to believe her.

'Fiancé? Since when have you been engaged? You don't wear a ring,' he pointed out accurately.

In reflex action, Mickey slipped her left hand into her pocket. 'I don't have one yet. We're keeping it a secret.'

Ryan's lip curled. 'So secret, you sound as if you don't know anything about it yourself! Where is this mystery man? Who is he?'

Feeling confident that her lies had worked once, she was only too happy to embroider. 'His name is Jack, and he's a pilot.'

Taking his weight on one leg, Ryan tucked his hands into his jeans pockets and eyed her consideringly. 'You never mentioned him before; why now?'

Because she'd never felt so threatened before. 'He's none of your business.'

'He must be some kind of man to get through that armour plating you wear, Hanlon. Or do you lower it for him? Do you melt for him?' he probed on silkily.

'You've a foul mind!' Mickey retorted disgustedly, and he smiled.

'It's considered normal to melt for the man you love and intend to marry, Hanlon. I think I've got to feel sorry for this fiancé of yours...if he exists.'

Cheeks flaming, Mickey glared at him. 'I'm telling you he exists. Why should I make him up?'

The smiled broadened. 'You tell me. OK, I'll give you the benefit of the doubt, but, just to be on the safe side, I'm going to be sleeping at your place tonight.'

Her gasp was audible. 'You will not!'

Ryan shook his head. 'Oh, but I will. Just in case you take it into your head to ring anyone who isn't your fiancé. But don't worry, I'll be sleeping on the couch. We wouldn't want you melting for the wrong man, would we?'

Words choked her. 'Why, you...you...!'

He didn't bother to listen, but walked to the door and held it open pointedly. 'After you, Hanlon,' he said, and waited.

Fuming impotently, Mickey stomped from the office, knowing it was useless to argue with him. The sight of his jeep in her rear-view mirror was like a probe in an open wound. He then had the gall to pull into her drive behind her, making it impossible for her to get her car out unless he moved his first.

Tasting defeat, Mickey climbed wearily from her car and walked to the front door of the single-storey house. She was tired and frustrated, and had the mother of all headaches. Switching on lights, she didn't bother to see what Ryan was doing; she knew he would be right behind her. In the lounge, she finally turned to face him.

His presence in the room was almost overpowering. He was too close, too big, too everything. She wanted him gone, but she knew it was a vain wish.

'Won't you need to go back to the hotel for a change of clothes?' she asked none the less, and got the answer she expected.

'I'll manage. Besides, I always keep a change of underwear in my bag.'

Pursing her lips, she pointed to a rather threadbare couch. 'You can make yourself comfortable on that. I'm going to have a bath, then go to bed.'

Ryan tossed his bag down beside the couch and frowned at her. 'Aren't you going to have something to eat?'

Right now, food would choke her. 'I'm not hungry, but you can help yourself to what you can find in the kitchen. Never let it be said I was a poor hostess! Now, if you'll excuse me?' She didn't wait to find out if he would or not, but went straight through to the bathroom and found some pain-killers in the medicine cabinet, washing them down with water. Only then did she glance at her reflection in the mirror. Not only did she look strained, but troubled, too.

Her hands gripped the edge of the sink until they were white-knuckled. Even here she could feel his alien presence in the house, taunting her. Even now, hate him though she did, she felt an urge to be with him, to be close to his vital source of energy. She groaned. Sexual energy, which lit her up inside like a neon sign.

She didn't want this, yet slowly but surely the compulsion was gaining in strength.

Mickey closed her eyes in despair. What was it he had said? That she could never outrun herself, only come to terms with who she was. But what if she didn't want to? What if she wanted to kill that thing inside her, but didn't know how? She had tried burying it, only to discover now, when it was far, far too late, that it had been a premature burial.

CHAPTER FIVE

MICKEY knew the instant she woke up that she was alone in the house. The electricity which had hummed in the air while Ryan was there had gone. Last night he had insisted she eat something, and had produced the fluffiest omelettes on her kitchen stove. To cap it all, she had actually enjoyed the food. She hadn't said so. She had been too angry at herself for finding she had missed the intimacy of sharing a meal with a man. Then, when she had gone to bed, expecting not to sleep with him in the house, she had been unable to keep her eyes open, not hearing a thing until her alarm went off.

It depressed her to realise one man could have such an effect on her, and it fitted her mood to discover it was raining. While she dressed, the heavy rain lessened to a persistent drizzle, which she knew from experience would hinder rather than help their search. Summer was over, and there was every possibility that the Misty Islands would be living up to their name, and other parts of the coast, too.

With that in mind, she layered her clothing, wearing a vest-type T-shirt next to her skin, then another of her plaid shirts, followed by a quilted body warmer. That way she could take off and put on according to the vagaries of the weather. The layers would also act as a barrier against Ryan's all too acute perception.

When she went through to the lounge, she discovered his makeshift bed had disappeared—and so had the telephone. He had had the incredible gall to take it away so that she wouldn't use it! In its place, a note written in strong handwriting informed her he expected her at the jetty by seven-thirty. Wishing it was him, she crumpled the note into a ball and threw it at the wall. Damn him. She had hoped Sophie would try to contact her, but now there was no chance of that.

Amelia was rocking gently at her moorings when a quietly simmering Mickey arrived at the shed, but she only noticed the fact in passing, her attention being on the noticeable absence of Ryan's jeep. She experienced the strangest feeling of disappointment. She had been keyed up to tell him exactly what she thought of him, but his absence irrationally deflated her. Irritably she told herself she was glad she had a small breathing space before facing him again—until she walked inside and was brought to an abrupt halt by the sight of him standing deep in conversation with Sid. He had rolled up his shirt-sleeves to reveal strong, tanned forearms, and was rubbing at oil-smeared hands with an equally oily cloth. Despite herself, her heart leapt, and she understood her earlier disappointment. She had wanted to argue with him just for the buzz it gave her. The knowledge hurt.

Seconds later her wayward heart danced even more crazily when, having sensed her presence, blue eyes swung round to lance into her. Then her breathing seemed to stop altogether when those same sapphire depths roved over her in lazily mocking appraisal before returning to her flushed face. He had known she was there all along, watching him. Feeling as if she were slowly falling to pieces, Mickey tried to deaden tingling nerves. When she could bring herself to speak, her voice fairly bristled with animosity, and not even she could have said if it was aimed entirely at Ryan Douglas.

'Your jeep isn't outside,' she snapped as he had a last word with the mechanic before walking towards her.

'It's round the back,' he informed her, halting a yard away and idly finishing his clean-up job. 'Any objections?'

In view of the fact that that was where he should have parked in the first place, there was no objection she could make without making even more of a fool of herself. So she ignored him, glancing to where Sid stood across the floor at the workbench, cleaning up his tools.

'Why are you here? What were you talking to Sid about?'

Resting his hands on his hips, Ryan shook his head sadly. 'Whatever happened to a simple "Good morning"? Especially when we've just spent the night together,' he rebuked her mockingly, 'and she felt heat sting her cheeks.

Mickey jammed her hands into the pockets of her body warmer. 'We did not spend the night together! And you still haven't said what you were doing,' she reminded him.

'Are you always this grouchy in the morning? Does Jack know? I'll have to remember to tell your fiancé to treat you very gently,' he declared sardonically.

Her teeth snapped together. 'Go to hell! And what have you done with my telephone?'

He grinned. 'I took it with me, in case you were tempted to call your..."fiancé". Your eyes have gone dark. I've noticed they tend to do that when you're angry...or aroused.'

She was both those. His eyes hadn't stopped regarding her with that lazy warmth, and, even as it stirred her blood, she knew he was doing it on purpose, and that made her angry. She wanted to hit him, to pummel her fists at him until he stopped, until he went away. But she didn't dare let go, for then he would know for certain that he was getting to her. With a strangulated moan, Mickey turned on her heel and marched away from him, going into her office and slamming the door behind her.

She came to a halt in the middle of the floor, fists clenched tightly at her sides, head bowed and eyes gripped shut in an effort to get control of her errant senses. She forced herself to take deep breaths, to relax tensed muscles, and finally allowed her eyes to open. Prosaically she noticed her shoelace had come undone. It seemed somehow symbolic, and she had to repress a ragged laugh. Automatically she lifted her foot on to a chair and bent to retie it. Before she could do so, however, she heard the door open and, glancing round, her eyes confirmed what her radar had already told her. Ryan stood in the doorway observing her.

'An interesting pose, but it would be much better if you were wearing black stockings and suspenders.'

Mickey straightened up instantly, the lace forgotten. 'Why must you say such things?' she demanded, and it was almost a despairing cry.

Walking inside, Ryan closed the door, soberly eyeing her rigid figure. 'Because you seem to expect it. I'm beginning to think you throw up that icy wall of yours simply to enjoy the pleasure of having a man break it down. I wouldn't be a man if I wasn't interested in finding out what was on the other side. Every now and again I get a glimpse of a passionate woman.'

Mickey's heart lurched. My God, was she doing that? Was she giving off signals saying, Here I am, come get me? Chilled, she knew she must be, for hadn't Jean-Luc claimed the same thing? Feeling diminished, she took refuge in anger. 'You're mistaken!' she snapped.

A softly sensuous smile curved his lips. 'I don't think so, Hanlon, but there's a sure way to find out,' he suggested, advancing on her in a manner that Mickey could only see as threatening.

Her heart leapt into her throat, and escape was the only thought in her head. 'I won't stay and listen to this!'

she declared thickly, and went to brush past him. Only she had forgotten the untied shoelace. As she attempted to move, the shoelace caught and she pitched forward with a startled cry of alarm.

She never did hit the ground, because two strong arms reached out to catch her, hauling her up close to a broad male chest. She found her face and hands pressed against his shirt, and, as she breathed in, the sheer male scent of him made her head spin. In a split second she was made vitally aware of the impressive strength of the arms which held her, of the muscled wall of his torso beneath her hands, and the accelerated sound of his heartbeat in her ear. Then she was dragged upwards, and her head fell back, and she found herself gazing helplessly into unfathomable blue eyes.

Everything faded away. Ryan's eyes blazed with the scent of victory as she moaned. As if the primal sound was a sign, his mouth found hers in a searing kiss that had no tender preliminaries. Nor, in that instant, would she have wanted anything less. All was heat and sensation, a burning, yearning need to know the taste, feel and essence of him. From a long way away Mickey heard someone making tiny whimpering noises, and realised it was herself. She welcomed the erotic thrust of Ryan's tongue and met it with her own. Her hands struggled to be free, then snaked around his neck, the fingers of one hand clenching into the deep curls of his hair, while the other clung on for dear life to his shirt.

Mindlessly the drugging kiss went on. As passion took over, she pressed herself ever closer to him, loving the feel of his hardness against her softness. There was a moment when Ryan hesitated, then his arms tightened instinctively, and they staggered backwards, stumbling into the wall, yet feeling no pain. He turned her then, pressing her against the wood and bringing his body tight against hers from thigh to chest, so that she could feel the strength of his arousal. She shivered as a wave of sensual heat swept through her, starting up a throbbing ache between her thighs.

Dear God, she wanted him. Wanted him as if there was nothing else of importance in the whole wide world!

Mickey tore her mouth free, dragging in air through a tight throat which arched as Ryan's lips plundered her frantic pulse. The firm glide of his hands down her back to her bottom, the way they held her and pulled her even closer to him, made her shiver deliciously. She closed her eyes as once again they staggered, leaving the wall, clinging, swaying to each other as another kiss devoured them.

This time it was Ryan who dragged his mouth away. The air was filled with the sound of their laboured breathing as they both strove to regain the control they had lost so tempestuously. Her body trembled in every limb, her lips felt bruised and tender, and there was an ache deep inside her that screamed to be satisfied. Mickey watched as Ryan raked visibly trembling hands through his hair—hair which, she recalled with a lurch of her heart, she had been responsible for mussing up.

Their eyes met. She didn't know what Ryan saw in her face, but she recognised the emotion on his. There was a scarcely banked desire, but, more notably, shock. It was this which caused Mickey to stumble backwards, careering into her desk and holding on to it as if it were a lifeline. The heat finally began to subside within her, and a dreadful sickness took its place. She had shocked him with her passion. Oh, he had wanted her, but that was purely in response to the way she had thrown herself at him. What man would refuse such a free gift? And she *had* been offering herself. How could she have done that? After all that had happened, how could she have allowed herself to want him like that? Want! She hammered the word into her mind. Want, not love. Never love.

With a stifled cry she turned away, staring sightlessly
at the litter on the desk. 'Get out!' The order was harsh,
and hurt her throat.

Ryan's gaze narrowed on her back. 'I think not. I think
we should talk.'

Driven over the edge, Mickey spun round, eyes glittering feverishly. She had to get him out of here, and
took the first course that offered itself. 'Look, I know
you think you've proved your point, but the truth of
the matter is I'm missing my fiancé. It wasn't you I was
kissing, but him. I'm not proud of it, but there's nothing
more to say. So I'd appreciate it if you'd just get out
and leave me alone!'

At her words a dangerous gleam entered his eyes and
his nostrils flared. 'Hold the phone, Hanlon! You're
saying I was just a convenient substitute to ease your
sexual frustration?' he shot back, striking home with a
vengeance.

It took Mickey an intense effort of will to remain upright when her legs threatened to collapse under her. 'You
heard correctly!' She wasn't prepared for any of this,
and now braced herself, crossing her arms, knowing she
had no other option than to go on. 'I'm sorry if I bruised
your ego!' How many insults would it take for him to
go? She longed to be alone, to lick her wounds.

There was an unpleasant twist to his lips as he stepped
back. 'You little bitch. Jack's welcome to you! I'll be
waiting out by the plane when you're ready.' He paused,
holding the door open, to send her one last scornful
smile. 'You're playing a dangerous game, Hanlon. You
come on hot like that with another man, and he might
not care that you aren't thinking of him. He'll just take
what's on offer anyway.'

He went with that, leaving Mickey to sag weakly
against the desk and bury her face in her hands. Oh,
God, she felt so cheap! The lies had been necessary, but
she hated herself for using them. Yet what else could

she have done? This was worse than before. Much, much worse. She hadn't responded to Jean-Luc with half the passion of those few kisses she had shared with Ryan. She had been so scared that, having discovered her response, he would want more—a brief affair to sate the senses—and then next week he would be gone, leaving her to pick up the pieces! Well, she wouldn't do it. She had been down that road, and it led nowhere, except to pain and humiliation. She might not have much, but she did have her pride, and she wasn't going to lose it again.

Which gave her the strength to straighten and stand up. OK, so she had belittled herself in Ryan's eyes, but it had had to be done. The danger hadn't passed. Even now she could still feel him and taste him. There was an addictiveness in his nearness which alarmed her, but only increased her determination not to give in to the dark side of her nature. She might, like her mother, be only capable of desiring, not loving, but she didn't have to indulge that trait.

This time when she bent to retie her shoelace she did so with firm, decisive movements. There was no time to ring a neighbour of Sophie's now; she would just have to continue the search as if nothing had changed. Who knew, perhaps they were looking in the right direction and would meet the runaways coming home? It was a slim chance, but one she clung to in the face of what she knew would be a far from comfortable day. She closed the door behind her and went to find her passenger, not noticing her hat lying abandoned on the floor.

Sid was waiting for her, but his face didn't bear his customary friendly smile. 'You shouldn't have lit into the fella like that, Mickey; he was only giving me a hand with the fuel pump. Came in early, too,' he reproved gruffly.

Mickey's eyes widened in surprise, then darted from the grizzled man at her side to the distant figure of Ryan as he waited by the float plane. 'He did?'

'Ain't afraid of getting his hands dirty, that's for sure. Seemed to enjoy it,' Sid went on with a respectful laugh, before angling a sly glance at her. 'Said he didn't like the idea of you flying about up there with a dodgy fuel supply.'

Mickey gasped as her nerves jolted violently, and turned puzzled eyes on her mechanic. 'Ryan said that?'

He squeezed her arm. 'Don't sound so surprised, girl. People do worry about you, those of us who care.'

A wave of warmth filled her at his obvious affection, but...Ryan care? That could hardly be true. She shrugged diffidently. 'He's probably thinking about his own neck,' she scoffed.

Sid tutted. 'That ain't worthy of you, Mickey. He's straight A and you know it.'

Was he? She was coming to think she didn't know anything any more. 'Did you find the trouble?' she asked, avoiding answering.

'Couldn't see anything, and it was working fine when we put it back. If it happens again, I'll put a new one in anyway.'

She nodded, although the thought of the cost lowered her spirits even more. 'OK, thanks, Sid. Well, I'd better be going. See you later.' With a brief wave she carried on her way.

Ryan straightened from his lounging position as she approached him, and Mickey braced herself for some acid remark, for his expression was chilly, but all he said was, 'Problems?'

It was a strange phenomenon, but, when she should have welcomed his coldness, she found she disliked it intensely, and that made no sense at all. Then common sense asserted itself. Although it hurt to be treated with contempt, it was definitely safer that way.

She raised her chin. 'If you must know, I was being told off for being angry with you when you were only trying to help,' she revealed honestly, then sighed heavily. 'You should have told me.'

He was wearing his hat and body warmer now, and stuffed his hands into the pockets. 'I got side-tracked,' he responded coldly. 'Are we ready to go now?'

She had been going to say more, but in the face of his withdrawal it was impossible to continue. 'Get in and I'll be with you in a few minutes. I take it we're still searching the Inside Passage?'

'Unless you've heard news to the contrary?' he challenged, eyes like gimlets checking for the slightest sign of deceit.

It was hard to believe that mere minutes ago they had been locked in a passionate embrace. 'The Passage it is, then,' she agreed, equally briskly, and turned away.

However, when they were safely airborne and well on their way to the point where they had called off the search last night, Mickey knew she had to return to the subject. It meant breaching the wall of silence she had been at pains to erect between them, but her conscience wouldn't let her rest until she made some amends.

'Ryan?' His name had a husky quality which sounded so good to her ears that it brought a pale hint of colour to her cheeks.

He looked round instantly. 'What is it? Have you seen something?'

She shook her head. Lord, would his eyes always have the ability to spear her to her soul? It was uncanny. 'No, I wanted to thank you.'

Surprise darkened his eyes for a moment, only to be displaced by derision. 'Thank me? Won't it stick in your craw?' he mocked.

It would if he kept up that attitude, but for the moment she held her temper in check. She kept her eyes fixed ahead of them, finding it easier that way. 'I want to thank you for helping Sid with the pump. And—er—I wanted to thank you for worrying about me, too.' She could feel

heat rising in her cheeks even as she made herself add
that last sentence.

'Don't go overboard, Hanlon. It was my neck I was
thinking about most,' Ryan discounted immediately.

They were virtually the same words she had used, but,
the minute he said them, she knew they were a lie. His
concern had been genuine. Straight A, as Sid had said.
She found she had a warm feeling in her stomach as she
glanced at him. 'All the same, I do thank you. I was
wrong to shout at you just because I thought you were
interfering,' she apologised huskily.

His laugh was derisory. 'Is that what you thought?'
he queried sardonically, and Mickey found herself
frowning as her heart suddenly increased its tempo.

'Why... yes.'

Laughing drily, Ryan shook his head. 'Get real,
Hanlon. You shouted at me for no other reason than
that I make you nervous.'

Her heart skipped a beat. 'Nonsense!'

To her dismay, his response was to reach over and put
his hand on her thigh. She jumped violently, and met
his cruelly amused blue eyes with her own shocked green
ones.

'As I said. I make you nervous.'

Mickey's throat had gone dry, and she swallowed
painfully. It hadn't been nerves which made her jump,
but the jolt of pleasure which had shot up her leg and
convulsed her stomach. Yet indirectly it was that very
reaction which did indeed make her nervous. As ever,
anger was her only means of defence.

'I jumped because I wasn't expecting you to touch
me!' she denied.

'After telling me I was only a substitute for your
fiancé, you mean?' he taunted harshly. 'Did my touch
remind you of Jack? Is that why you enjoyed it? Or are
you nervous now because you enjoyed my touch and it
didn't remind you of him?' Ryan challenged, holding

her shocked gaze. 'You have very expressive eyes, Hanlon.'

She couldn't look away, even though it was dangerous in more ways than one to keep her eyes locked with his. There was a strange smile on his lips as he reached over and covered her hand with his large, strong one, easing the stick back slightly, giving them more height.

'Do you want to know what they're saying now?' he asked softly, invitingly, and oh, so seductively.

Her throat closed over, and she seemed helpless to do anything other than let him take control. 'Ryan...I...' Her voice was a croak which petered out altogether.

'They're telling me I scare you, but I thrill you too.' He tipped his head. 'They're telling me not to stop...but being used as a pinch-hitter for your Jack has no more appeal now than it did half an hour ago. So I must decline the offer. When I make love to a woman I want to know she's with me all the way, not thinking of some other man. And you are thinking of another man, aren't you, Hanlon?' Leaving that mocking question hanging in the air between them, he moved away, settling back in his seat and studying the world below them.

Mickey blinked, shuddering as she came out of that near state of trance, very much aware that he could have done anything and she would not have stopped him. Horrified, she stared ahead, knowing she had been lost to the world when her concentration should have been at its most aware. The hot press of tears behind her eyes was a sign of her self-disgust. Ryan had been right about her reaction, and he had just got his pound of flesh. She should have known that he wasn't the sort of man to let a slur on his manhood go unpunished. More to the point, he now knew she had been lying.

Feeling wretched, Mickey brought the float plane back down to a suitable level for their search. She was a weak fool, and, like a fool, she had allowed him to manipulate her. All because she hadn't been able to control herself!

'Don't take it so badly, Hanlon. You never were a saint, just human like the rest of us.' His ironic rejoinder was tossed casually over his shoulder as he continued his search.

Her eyes shot daggers into him. 'You're not human; you're an animal!' she retorted, loading the declaration with all the loathing she felt.

Now he did look at her, but he was amused, not angry. 'Animals mate, they don't make love. When I take you to bed, you'll find out the difference.'

The statement was meant to shock her, and it did. What did he mean? Had it not been punishment enough to make her give herself away? Did he intend to extract a more poignant revenge, by making love to her? She bit her lip. He could do it too, because her instinctive alarm was tinged with something else which melted her insides. She recognised it as desire, and hated herself for it.

Suddenly she felt she was in the middle of a fight to the death, and it was a losing battle! But she couldn't afford to lose. Valiantly she sought for a way of routing him, some way to put some distance between them so that he wouldn't be tempted to carry out any plans he might have. The answer was not long in coming. She had to make him despise her even more, and she had the very means to do so.

'Yesterday you said you wanted me to take you to Leah and Peter. Well, I've thought it over, and I'll take you to them, for a price,' she declared suddenly, and the statement echoed around the cockpit.

Ryan's head turned sharply. 'You'll what?' he asked incredulously, eyes narrowing on her pale, set features.

Mickey forced herself to look right at him. 'I'll take you to them for a quarter of a million dollars,' she repeated baldly, and saw shock warring with a mounting anger on his face.

'You mean you've known where they are all along? My God, you hard-nosed little . . . You were just holding out for the right price, weren't you?' he charged contemptuously, and her throat closed over.

She didn't admit anything. 'Is it a deal?'

Ryan shook his head slowly. 'I thought I'd seen everything, but you're something else. OK, it's a deal. Turn this crate around and take me there, and, so help me, if this is another of your games . . . Just get me there, Hanlon,' he finished grimly, and it was all she could do to hold back a scalding flood of tears. The alienation was complete.

Mickey banked the plane and headed back home. She would take him to Sophie, who must have news of Leah and Peter by now. It was all she could think of to do. The wind, which had freshened, seeing off the last of the drizzle, dropped again. As soon as it did so, the mist began to close in once more, and visibility began to deteriorate rapidly. Then, as luck would have it, the engine began to play up, and finally stopped altogether.

'Another game, Hanlon?' Ryan taunted harshly, and she glared at him.

'I only wish it were!' she denied with feeling. She wasn't alarmed, although it was an anxious time as she tried everything she knew to get the craft started again. Finally she gritted her teeth. 'It's no good; I'm going to have to take her down.'

Ryan nodded, not wasting time asking useless questions. 'OK. There's a bay over here that looks promising. If we have to stay the night, it's at least got some beach and a bit of protection.'

Mickey didn't argue, but banked the float plane and let her glide down, taking her in as far as she could before landing on the water, because they had no engine to help taxi to the shore. Fortunately their own momentum carried them to the beach, and, without waiting for directions, Ryan was letting himself out of the door, jumping on to the float and then into the shallows, using the mooring line to pull the plane closer before tying her off to a conveniently fallen tree.

Mickey climbed out after him, shivering a little at the clammy feel of the air. She negotiated the float agilely, then hesitated as Ryan reached up his arms to help her down.

'No use both of us getting wet feet, Hanlon,' he told her sensibly, and, knowing it was true, she placed her hands on his shoulders and let him take her round the waist and swing her down.

There was no reason why her heart should be in her throat, but that was where it ended up as her feet touched the ground. Beneath her hands his body was warm, and her fingers had a tendency to want to linger, so she forced them to let go, stepping back and causing his hands to drop away from her. There was cynical amusement in the curve of his mouth when she shot him a glance.

'Thanks.'

'You're welcome.' Ryan was coolly polite. 'Are any of these islands inhabited?'

Mickey shrugged and dragged a hand through her hair. 'Some, I guess, but don't ask me which. Mostly folks come out by boat and go back again. The islands are beautiful by daylight, but they can be creepy at night.'

'Then you'd better hope we can manage to fix whatever's wrong, or we'll be spending the night here and finding out how creepy they are for ourselves.'

She turned away, vowing she'd make the repairs if it killed her. 'I'm going to contact Sid on the radio, tell him what happened and where we are. If we can't get Amelia going, he'll have to come out for us.' Hang the cost, this was a real emergency, and the plane was only half of it.

Ryan remained silent for a few seconds, but when she refused to look at him a grim expression settled on to his face. 'You do that. While the engine cools, I'll gather up some of this driftwood. We might need it before the day is over.'

As she clambered back on to the float, she hoped not, because the idea of spending the night out here alone with Ryan was something she simply hadn't bargained for, and was to be avoided at all costs.

Mickey brushed a tired hand over her brow and left a streak of oil behind. She was too frustrated to care. During the last few hours they had tried every permutation they could think of, but each time they tried to restart the engine the result was the same—failure. Now, to cap it all, she had just got off the radio asking for Sid to come and get her, only to be told the mist had turned to fog, and nothing would be taking off tonight. The earliest he could reach them was tomorrow morning, and he couldn't specify a time.

Looking out of the window, she could see the mist had thickened quite considerably while they worked. She could also see Ryan over by the pile of wood he had gathered earlier. He was building a fire with the ease of long experience. She watched him work with a fateful fascination. She had said things to make him back off, but it hadn't stopped the temptation she felt. It seemed to make no difference that he was rich and good-looking, and treated women like toys, just like Jean-Luc.

She closed her eyes. He was making her want things she knew it was bad to covet, because they had no value outside a fleeting satisfaction. And when it was over, what then? Could she rebuild all over again, or would it be too late? Once she had awakened the tiger, it might refuse to go back into its cage. It might demand to have its hunger appeased again and again, going endlessly on a search for something it never found, just like her mother.

She shuddered, then jumped violently as a hand pressed down on her shoulder. Her eyes shot open, and she stared blankly up at Ryan as he loomed over her in the cramped cockpit.

'You OK, Hanlon?' The concern in his voice sounded genuine, and the gentle kneading of his fingers was a silent comfort, but Mickey was so alarmed by her own thoughts that her response was as hot as her cheeks became.

'I thought you were building a fire,' she charged, and didn't know if she felt relieved or not when he immediately released her and straightened up.

'I was,' he agreed levelly. 'I came in to ask if you had some matches. When I saw you slumped in the chair, I was naturally concerned, and it made me forget you don't like me touching you,' he gibed, and the mockery was all the more potent because they both knew the truth.

Mickey paled. Not like him touching her? What would he say if he knew that it was precisely because she had been imagining him doing more than just touching her that she had reacted so sharply? Lord, she had never met anyone who made her emotions swing so violently as this man, so that she was always in danger of betraying herself!

'There's nothing wrong, unless you count that Sid can't get to us because of the fog. We're stuck here for the night,' she explained brusquely. It was the only way she could get the words out.

Ryan propped himself against the other seat. 'The prospect failed to please? Knowing you, as I'm coming to, I can't say I'm surprised. What's going to worry you more—that I will pounce, or that I won't? Poor Hanlon, you can't bear to be here, but I'll have you know there are women who would give a fortune to be in your shoes right now.'

Mickey ground her teeth. Trust him to go for the jugular! 'Did they all escape from the same asylum?' she gibed, and wished she hadn't when he uttered that laugh again which curdled her insides.

When he stopped, he tutted. 'Anyone listening to you would imagine a woman had to be mad to get involved with me.'

Her lip curled. 'Surely no sane woman would choose to be used that way,' she countered tartly, and one eyebrow arched at her.

'Tell me, Hanlon, just how do you imagine I use women?' Ryan challenged softly. 'I don't abuse them, either physically or mentally, nor do I treat them like empty-headed nitwits.'

'Big deal!' she scoffed. 'They're still mere objects to you, to be used for your pleasure and then to be cast aside when you grow bored!'

Ryan looked amused as he crossed his arms. 'You've been reading too much gossip, Hanlon. If I'd bedded all the women the papers say I have I'd have been dead years ago! Strange as the concept may seem to you, I don't take women out simply to go to bed with them. I have more respect for them and for myself. Yes, I have had affairs, but only with women for whom I have a great deal of regard. The others were just window-dressing, because most of the functions I have to attend require that I have a partner.

'Mostly I take women out because I enjoy their company. In most cases I enjoy their brains and not their bodies. I enjoy intelligent conversation wherever I can get it, and there are one hell of a lot of intelligent women out there. The fact that many of them are beautiful too is a bonus. I'm no sexual athlete. I have neither the time nor the inclination.'

The revelation surprised her. She had been utterly convinced she knew what type of man he was. Now he was telling her what she really should have known—that the tabloids had added embroidery to invention, and her own experiences had done the rest. Logic alone should have told her that no man who spent his life crossing and recrossing the globe could be at all as he was portrayed. There just wasn't time. Nor could anyone with the insight his photographs showed he had treat women so cheaply. Life was precious to him, all life.

She had done him an injustice, even if only in her thoughts, and owed him an apology. 'I'm sorry. I can't stand gossip. I don't know why I listened to it,' she said stiffly, only to receive a derisory laugh in reply.

'Because it gave you a valid reason not to like me,' he enlightened her with heavy irony.

Sweet heaven, he cut through to the truth like a hot knife through butter! 'I still don't like you!'

Producing a handkerchief from his pocket, he handed it to her. 'You've got oil on your forehead,' he informed her, watching her rub at the offending streak before carrying on. 'Now you don't like me because you want me, and you've nothing to hide behind.'

Mickey's nerves fluttered wildly, and she thrust his handkerchief back at him with a hand which trembled. 'I don't want you!'

Ryan's lips curved contemptuously. 'You'd rather I thought that your response to me this morning was out of frustration? That any man would have done?' There was a hard edge to the taunt as his blue gaze narrowed on her pale face.

Mickey choked on a reply. If she said yes, what did that make her? But she couldn't say no. She desperately wanted to resort to violence, but that would get her short shrift from this man, and possibly the sort of retaliation she simply wouldn't be able to handle. This man didn't use his hands, because he had much stronger weapons at his disposal.

'You're loathsome,' she finally managed to splutter.

'Because I'm forcing you to face the truth about yourself?' he taunted as he pushed himself upright again.

Her stomach lurched sickeningly. The truth? He had no concept of what the truth meant! 'Go to hell!' she grated defensively, and he laughed.

'Predictable to the last. OK, Hanlon, have it your way. You'd better point me in the direction of the matches before the wood gets too damp to light,' he said prosaically, and she was grateful for a return to normality.

She pointed to a box. 'Over there. You'll find water and the emergency rations. There should be blankets, too. We can curl up by the fire for warmth.' Ryan had supplied another hamper, but they'd eaten most of that at lunchtime, when they'd still had hopes of repairing the plane.

He found everything as she spoke and sent her a sardonic look. 'For a minute there I thought you were going to suggest we share body warmth to save ourselves. But you'd rather freeze to death, wouldn't you, Hanlon?' he taunted, and climbed out again.

She stared after him, knowing it wasn't true. It hadn't been true from the moment he'd walked into her office, and that was what scared her most.

CHAPTER SIX

'ALL the comforts of home,' Ryan declared drily when Mickey joined him, having unearthed a can of vegetable soup, a tinned meat pie and a can of peaches, together with camping saucepans, can opener and cutlery. 'You travel well prepared, which begs the question, do you get stranded often?'

'Only when I don't have enough money to make proper repairs,' she snapped back instantly, and regretted it when she looked up to find herself being observed by a pair of chilly blue eyes.

His smile was equally cold. 'Well, when you take me to Peter you'll be laughing, won't you?'

Mickey couldn't hold his gaze as the lie brought colour to her cheeks. She didn't think she'd ever feel like laughing again. 'I could do with the money,' she mumbled, and picked up a can.

Ryan sat back on his heels. 'That's quite an admittance, coming from you, Hanlon. Here, let me do that.' He held out his hands for the tins and opener.

'I can manage,' she protested, but he reached across and took them from her anyway.

'Don't go all feminine on me, Hanlon, I might faint from shock.' With an economy of movement he speared a tin and began to cut.

Mickey found herself watching his hands. He had long fingers, indicting the artist in him, but they were capable too. She found herself wondering what it would feel like to have them on her body, stroking her. Would he be as sensitive with female flesh as he was with his camera, drawing the soul from her? The thought made her body temperature rise, and, hidden from view, her nipples peaked, almost as if they had experienced the brush of his fingers over them.

Something popped in the fire, making her jump and bringing her to her senses. What was she doing? Dear lord, how could she be having such erotic thoughts when he was simply opening a tin of soup?

'So what brought you to Canada?'

She had been so caught up in her own thoughts that she only heard the words and not their meaning. She was left blinking at him like an idiot, colour washing into her cheeks as he paused from his task to look at her, eyebrows shooting skywards as he witnessed her shock. Mickey caught an arrested expression in his eyes before his lids lowered.

'Keep staring at me like that, Hanlon, and I might get the idea the menu is even more varied than I thought.'

Her heart gave an almighty lurch. Surely he couldn't see what she had been thinking? The idea was appalling, and she felt her cheeks pale. 'I wasn't looking at you!' she protested, and received a mocking look for her pains.

'I know. You were just thinking of your fiancé, and getting the two of us mixed up again. You'd better do something about that before the wedding, or you might just start calling him Ryan!' he taunted.

Mickey drew an angry breath and forgot prudence. 'I've never mixed you up!' she protested vigorously, and then realised the enormity of her mistake.

Ryan's teeth gleamed whitely as he smiled unpleasantly. 'No, you just like to tease, don't you, sweetheart? To turn the screw. Well, I'm on to you now, and the next time you give me the come-on don't expect me to back off.'

Choked, she found it impossible to sit beside him a moment longer. Rising agitatedly, she covered the short distance to the water's edge on unsteady legs.

The water didn't look at all inviting, but it was what she needed right now. She didn't hesitate. Stripping off her body warmer and shirt, Mickey found a large handkerchief in her pocket and dunked it in the icy water. She needed a wash, and she needed to cool off, too. Though it brought her out in goose-bumps, she religiously moistened every inch of bare flesh, squeezing the cloth at her throat so that an icy trickle ran down between her breasts. It had the effect she wanted, and gradually her hot blood cooled.

She was just congratulating herself on getting back in control, when, in a few telling words, all the good was undone.

'Well, well, well, I always guessed there must be a woman underneath that camouflage you wear, Hanlon, but even I didn't know it would be so curvaceous and alluring. Or that you don't bother with a bra,' Ryan's strangely husky voice declared from behind her.

With a gasp she looked over her shoulder, realising too late that her every move had been highlighted by the fire. Angrily she reached for her shirt, shrugging it on over damp skin with jerky movements.

'You could have had the decency to look away,' she berated him in a choked, stifled voice as she fumbled into the body warmer, but even the thickness of that couldn't wipe out the feeling that he could now see through every layer to her skin!

'If you didn't want me to look, you should have gone out of the firelight altogether,' Ryan countered smoothly, and embarrassment made her see red.

'So it's me in the wrong, not you?' Mickey spluttered wrathfully.

He didn't answer for a moment, and his steady gaze was almost unnerving. 'Why so het up? You weren't naked—far from it,' he pointed out, with the sort of logic she couldn't fault.

The trouble was, although she hadn't been naked, he had made her feel as if she were. Now, hating to feel this open and vulnerable, she fired the first weapon which came to hand. 'I have the right not to be ogled!'

He laughed, but when she remained standing stiffly before him Ryan's face became deadly serious in the flickering firelight. 'Are you ashamed of your body? Is that why you cover it up in these shapeless clothes?'

Mickey gritted her teeth, her breathing ragged at the sharpness of his mind. 'No, I am not ashamed of my body. I simply choose not to draw attention to it!'

A slight frown creased his forehead as he tried to probe into her mind. 'Why? As far as I could judge, you have a very beautiful body,' he argued quietly.

The simple statement took the fight right out of her, and she could only stare at him helplessly, raking a hand through her short hair. Crazy as it seemed, to know he found her beautiful made her feel warm inside. Yet she couldn't allow herself to enjoy it. 'Well, perhaps I don't want a beautiful body!' she finally pronounced lamely.

'Too late, sweetheart, you've got one, and hiding it won't make it disappear,' he pointed out logically.

Mickey hugged her arms around herself. Turbulent green eyes raked him. 'Did it ever occur to you that what you find beautiful might seem a curse to someone else?'

Now he frowned heavily. 'And you feel cursed? Is that why you came to Canada and hid yourself away? What happened?'

If he hadn't added that last question, the truth might have come tumbling from her lips, but just in time she remembered who he was, and why it was so very important that she build up her defences, not weaken them from within. She withdrew into herself, dropping down beside the fire once more and making a show of preparing the food.

'I came to Canada to find my father, nothing more shocking than that. Er—I think I'll add water to the soup—it will make it go further—but I can boil the tinned pie using sea water.' As she spoke she began shuffling pans until Ryan's hand on hers halted her.

'Silence can be seen as an admission, not a denial!'

For once his touch didn't faze her. 'Presupposing there was anything to tell, give me one good reason why I should tell you, Ryan.'

Irritation flared in his eyes. 'I can think of a quarter of a million good reasons. Hell, you need the money. Think what you could do with half a million!' he exploded, and she blanched, feeling faint with shock.

'You think I'd tell you for money?' she charged in distaste.

'Isn't that how you operate?' Ryan challenged tersely as he released her. 'Money for information. You've already accepted once, so you can't suddenly tell me my money isn't good enough.'

'I'll never think anything that comes from you is good,' she told him bluntly, even as she knew her own actions had laid her open for his claim. It really shouldn't hurt when he used it against her, but it did.

There was a speculative gleam in Ryan's eye at that. 'Nothing?' he taunted. 'Not even my kisses?'

Mickey's heart skipped a beat, but she didn't look away from him. 'Especially those!' she snapped, and couldn't hold back a gasp as he suddenly rose to his feet.

'You know something, Hanlon, I'm going to make you eat those words one day,' he promised as he took the largest pan and bent down to fill it with water, leaving Mickey staring at his back.

She bit her lip, almost drawing blood. This was the last thing she needed. Every time she tried to rebuild her defences, he simply made a hole somewhere else. He stood up, and she hastily bent over the soup, stirring like crazy.

'Leave some tin on the bottom, won't you?' Ryan advised mockingly, forcing her to look up again.

'Very funny!'

He squatted down, fitting the pan of water over the heat. After a moment he sighed. 'Listen, Hanlon. We're both tired and hungry, and we're both stuck here, like it or not. The way I see it, we have two choices. We can keep up this war of words to the bitter end, or we can declare a truce. I'm for the latter, but the decision is up to you.'

Mickey looked at him dubiously, unsure whether to accept or not. But there was no denying she was exhausted. It would be lovely to lay down her arms for a while. So long as he kept his distance, everything would be all right.

'OK. A truce,' she agreed huskily, and prayed to God she wouldn't regret it!

Mickey drained the last drip of coffee from her mug and wondered at the contrariness of fate which had made Ryan Douglas the ideal companion in adversity. She didn't know exactly how he had done it, but they had shared a most relaxing meal. Considering she had been at daggers drawn with him two hours ago, it was a minor miracle. Perhaps it had something to do with the stories he had regaled her with as they ate, tales of the hazards of foreign travel, and filming in the strangest of places and situations.

She hadn't expected him to have a sense of humour, but discovered he had an ability to laugh at himself which she couldn't help but admire. There were other things to admire, too, things which came across, probably without his knowledge—like his concern and compassion for those less fortunate than himself. But she had already gleaned that from his photographs.

As the night deepened, she very soon came to the conclusion that Ryan Douglas the photographer was a man she could like and respect. But Ryan Douglas the man was someone she didn't dare let herself like. To do so would threaten the whole fabric of her life, and she had worked so hard to build it up. It made her feel strangely empty inside to acknowledge that they could never be friends. Even if he gave a sign that he might want to be, it would be safer for her if they weren't.

'You've gone very quiet,' Ryan observed. 'Have I bored you to sleep?'

'Oh, I'm not bored,' Mickey denied quickly, too quickly to be altogether casual, and, recognising it, she hastened to cover herself. 'I was just thinking it must be nice to be able to pick and choose the work you want to do. You must get commissions which take you all over the world,' she ventured, hugging her arms around her knees to ward off an ever increasing chill in the air.

Ryan gave a half-smile. 'It's never dull. For instance, from here I'll be heading off to Europe. A friend of mine has asked me to do the illustrations for his latest book. He's an archaeologist, and gets withdrawal symptoms if he isn't grubbing about in Greek earth.'

Mickey's head came up, her look wistful. 'I'd give a fortune to be able to swap places with him for five minutes!' she exclaimed.

She had intrigued him. 'I thought you were wedded to your planes.'

Mickey shook her head. 'Only partly. My father taught me to love flying, and I wouldn't give it up now, but my first love was history. I wanted to go to university and study archaeology.' The animation gradually died out of her face as she recalled that time in her life.

Across from her, Ryan stretched out beside the fire, making himself more comfortable. 'Why didn't you?' he probed.

She pulled a rueful face. As a teenager, she hadn't had the strength of will to fight for her own future. 'I was needed at home. My mother needed me,' she qualified, knowing it was no more true now than it had been then.

Filial duty had weighed heavily on her slim shoulders, and even now she couldn't be disloyal.

'She was an invalid?'

Ryan's question surprised her, although it was a logical conclusion to make. 'No. She's always been ruggedly healthy. It was me. I suppose I was a rather insecure teenager, and when my mother said she needed me...well, that seemed more important.'

'Yet you left anyway,' he pointed out, and, after the briefest of pauses, added softly, 'What happened to make you change your mind?'

Her nerves leapt, and she gave him a narrow-eyed look, meeting a bland one in return. Indignation seethed inside her. Lord, he had been clever, using her own reminiscences against her. Fortunately her antennae hadn't gone completely to sleep, and she backed off from the dangerous edge of the precipice.

She smiled thinly. 'Let's just say I finally saw the way my life was going, and I didn't like it.'

The inclination of his head was a silent *touché*. 'And that's when you came looking for your father? Did your mother know?' Ryan probed on notwithstanding.

So much for the truce, Mickey thought waspishly. 'She helped me find him. Their divorce was quite amicable. I'm sorry if the lack of family friction disappoints you,' she finished tersely.

He sent her another of those long looks he was so good at. 'I'm not disappointed. I'm always happy for anyone who comes out of a divorce unscathed. Is your mother still alive? Do you keep in contact with her?'

Mickey sighed, knowing she only had herself to blame for opening a crack in the first place. However, she was determined this wasn't going to turn into true confessions! 'I write regularly. It wasn't a condition of my going, but something I do because I love my mother. We just don't have the same outlook on life, that's all.' Which was why those letters contained white lies to keep

Tanita happy and stop her from worrying, because, despite the way it might look to outsiders, the actress loved her daughter too.

'And what of the future? Don't you plan to get married and have a family of your own?'

The question caught her on the raw, for once such an outcome had seemed the inevitable goal of her life. Events since had caused her to wise up. Now she laughed, and there was an edge of cynicism to it. 'Can you really see me wallowing in domesticity, with children clinging to my skirt?'

'Strangely enough I can,' Ryan admitted, making her chin drop.

An enormous lump seemed to have materialised in her throat. 'I'm a professional woman!' she pointed out thickly.

'That doesn't necessarily preclude you from having a family. Many women successfully juggle career and family,' Ryan argued neatly, then shot a devastating arrow at her heart. 'Don't you want to fall in love, Hanlon?'

Feeling as if she was under attack and not sufficiently armed to protect herself, she answered scornfully, 'Falling in love is a fairy-tale, and I never did care much for them.'

Ryan found a chink in her armour at the first attempt. 'Some man did quite a job on you, didn't he?'

Mickey felt as if all her defences were slowly being stripped away. Desperately she sought to cover up. 'Don't be ridiculous!'

'Your reaction tells me I'm not being ridiculous, sweetheart. When a passionate woman says love doesn't exist, you can bet there's a man involved.'

'That's not true!' she spluttered, wishing she felt angry, but experiencing only a pervasive despair.

Blue eyes narrowed. 'What isn't true? That you're a passionate woman, or that there was a man? The former

I can disprove right away, so what you are denying is the existence of a man in your past.'

Mickey found she had been gripping a large pebble, and now she vented her anger by throwing it into the fire, sending a shower of sparks skywards. 'All right! There was a man I thought I loved, but I was wrong. And you're wrong in thinking he made me not believe in love. It exists all right, just not for me.'

Ryan's frown deepened. 'You're rather young to be making that sort of statement. Who knows what's around the next corner?'

She laughed, a harsh sound which hurt her throat. 'If it was the man of my dreams, I'd walk right past him!'

There was a stillness in him now, a waiting. 'Too scared to take another chance?' It was almost a taunt, and yet not quite.

Mickey had no hesitation in shaking her head, and a wistful smile curved her lips. 'Love doesn't scare me,' she revealed, and quite clearly heard his intake of breath.

'Something does,' Ryan pursued doggedly, although it was clear her reply had surprised him.

She looked him in the eye. 'Perhaps. But life is a matter of choices, isn't it? We all make them every day. I don't have to be scared of the things I choose not to do.'

'Can you make that sort of decision about love?'

Her brows rose. 'Haven't you? You aren't married either, are you?' she countered immediately.

Ryan relaxed again, smiling faintly. 'You're right, Hanlon; we do make choices. I could have married, but I chose to wait until I found the woman I loved. For security or companionship, or simply to have children of my own, I could have married years ago. But I'm greedy; I want it all. I want the grand passion or none at all,' he confessed easily, but, for all that, she knew he meant every word.

For a moment she experienced a warm feeling about her heart. That was why her next question made her feel sad. 'But what if the woman you love doesn't love you?'

'Inconceivable!'

She couldn't help but laugh at that. 'What conceit!'

He wagged a finger at her. 'Not conceit, Hanlon, self-protection. I have to believe she'd feel the same, or there would be no point in carrying on the search.'

'And if you never find her?'

'Never is a long time. I'll find her, you can bet on it.'

'Meanwhile, you'll take your fun where you find it?'

He tutted. 'Don't sound so disapproving. There's nothing wrong in dating women. I'm a red-blooded man; what else would you expect? But I'm not in a continual state of rut, and I always make sure I play by the rules and do my best not to hurt anyone.'

Mickey grimaced. 'And of course that makes everything all right!'

Ryan shrugged. 'At least I don't go around telling people I'm thinking of someone else when I'm holding them. That was a low blow, Hanlon.'

Guilty colour washed into her cheeks. 'I didn't ask you to kiss me,' she retorted swiftly, aware that her heart rate had accelerated again.

'Tell that to the marines!' Ryan scoffed, watching the play of emotions over her face with interest. 'You were with me all the way, until you suddenly got cold feet. It took me a while to realise you'd thrown up another smoke-screen. You use words like weapons. But you didn't have to shoot me down, Hanlon. What happened took us both by surprise. You only had to tell me I was going too fast for you.'

Mickey ground her teeth in frustration. She was back where she had started from, with the ground neatly cut from under her. 'I'd rather tell you to go to hell!'

Firelight glittered in his eyes, turning them deep and mysterious. 'Words are cheap, Hanlon. I'm more interested in what happens when I touch you. Want to try best of three?'

How she would love to say yes, and prove him wrong by freezing him off, but the way her flesh heated up at the mere thought of kissing him told her she would most surely lose. 'Why don't you just think of all the reasons why you dislike me?' she snapped instead.

'It's a funny thing, Hanlon, but when I think of you in my arms I can't remember a single one of them!' Ryan declared outrageously, leaving her fuming impotently.

'Strange, but that only recalls all the reasons why I loathe you!' Mickey returned waspishly.

'Say it often enough, and—who knows?—it may finally become true. You don't loathe me; you want me.'

It was his damned matter-of-factness which galled her so. He didn't even doubt it, and any denial she made would be, as he knew, just words. 'Why are you doing this?'

'Why do you think?' he countered blandly, and she could have screamed.

'Because it amuses you. Because you can't stand to see even one woman get away! Even if, by your own description, she's not much of a woman in the first place!' Mickey rejoined, and was dismayed to hear how hurt she sounded.

Ryan pulled a wry face. 'I was angry when I said that. I've since discovered that there's more to you than meets the eye. I keep getting glimpses of an intriguing, passionate woman. I'd like to meet her. Something tells me she'll be worth knowing.'

Mickey simply didn't know how to handle a man as persistent as this. She could only resort to sarcasm. 'Why bother to dress it up? All you want to do is get her into bed!'

'It could be quite an experience.'

'So is climbing Everest, but I've no intention of doing either!' Mickey scorned, trying to still a racing pulse.

'To think, three days ago I didn't even know you! I didn't know I could detest anyone so quickly!'

Ryan climbed agilely to his feet. 'We're learning all the time, and if we don't soon move we'll be finding out what pneumonia is like. I suggest we leave the washing-up until morning and get back into the plane.'

Mickey stood up slowly. 'I thought we were going to sleep by the fire.' To share the cramped conditions of the aircraft with him would be putting herself too close to temptation.

Ryan merely waved a hand at the mist which now swirled about them. 'Another hour out here and we'd be soaked through. Even you wouldn't be that foolish, Hanlon. Or don't you trust yourself alone with me?'

It was just the taunt to have her girding her loins. 'Don't flatter yourself! It's obvious you've never tried sleeping in a float plane, or you'd know how uncomfortable it was. The seats aren't designed for it, and there's not what you'd call much floor space,' she invented quickly, although the description was dismayingly accurate.

Ryan made his way round to her side. 'It's nice to know you feel concerned for my welfare, Hanlon, but I'll grit my teeth and bear it if you will.'

Damn it, he was laughing at her! 'Oh, well, I once had to share with a prize pig, so I guess I can put up with you for one night!' she riposted blightingly, only to hear him laugh outright as he followed her down to the water's edge.

'You have interesting ways of giving a man a put-down, Hanlon. Must be all those years of practice. Trouble is, my skin's so thick, all you'll do is blunt yourself against it. What happens when you're defenceless?'

Mickey clambered up on to the float before turning to look down at him. 'I'll rely on the fact that you're a gentleman, and would never do anything against a lady's

will,' she said sweetly, and he inclined his head in acknowledgement of a hit.

'Very good, Hanlon. Either I do as you say or prove
I'm no gentleman. Yet I'm only human. What if my
passion proves stronger than my gallantry? Or your will
proves to be made of straw? Now there's a thought to
see us through the long, cold night,' Ryan ventured as
he joined her.

Mickey had had enough. 'Oh, shut up!' she ordered,
and turned her back on him to enter the darkened aircraft. She wished she had the nerve to lock him out in
the cold, but her conscience wouldn't let her do it.

There wasn't much room for manoeuvre, but in the
space they had Mickey spread out her blanket and made
a pillow out of her body warmer. She didn't look to see
what Ryan was doing, but kept her back to him as she
removed her boots and lay down, wrapping the blanket
around her.

'You know, we really would be warmer sharing the
blankets, Hanlon,' Ryan observed.

'We'll be fine once you've closed the door,' she countered hardily, and after a moment heard the lock being
set. After that there was a lot of activity as he made up
his own bed and climbed into it, making himself
comfortable.

'Goodnight, Hanlon,' Ryan murmured from right
behind her, making her nerves flutter wildly.

She tensed immediately, feeling the warmth of him,
knowing she only had to turn to be in his arms. And
with the night all around them, she finally admitted to
herself that that was where she wanted to be. Safe in his
embrace. But she knew also that that was a contra-
diction in terms, and moved as far away from him as
she could.

'Night,' she responded gruffly, willing herself to go to
sleep quickly, but it wasn't till long after the sound of

Ryan's breathing told her he was asleep that she finally relaxed enough to follow suit.

She was having a dream. One of those where you didn't know whom or what you were running from, or to. She tried to call out, and it was the indeterminate sounds of her moans which roused Ryan. He turned in the gloom to see her threshing about, and reached over to shake her.

Mickey came awake with a cry, shuddering as she recalled the anxiety of her dream. Her heart was racing, and in that moment of stress it was the most natural thing in the world to turn to the man beside her and be drawn into a pair of secure, strong arms.

'Shush. Relax. You're OK now,' Ryan murmured into her hair, his hand running soothingly down her back.

Mickey knew she had never felt more OK in her life, and the feeling beat back the dark coils of her dream. Clinging to his shirt, she buried her face in his neck, shuddering as the tendrils released her.

'You were dreaming. Want to tell me what it was about?' he offered, but she shook her head.

'I don't want to think about it.'

'OK, honey, relax. I've got you safe,' Ryan soothed, and the movement of his lips was a caress on her neck.

She should have frozen, but didn't, and in an instant it seemed her mind was filled with nothing else but the sensation of that almost-kiss. It felt good, and her instinct was to press herself closer to his warm male body. In fact, she must have done so, for he kissed her again, finding a sensitive cord which had her arching her neck as a sigh escaped her softly parted lips. One of her hands came up to gently maraud its way across broad, cloth-covered shoulders, delighting in their strength, yet feeling a growing irritation at being denied a closer contact.

A small voice told her this was dangerous, but, with her defences lowered to the point of non-existence, she

argued that she would stop in a moment. She would
just... Digging her fingers into silken hair, she levered
his head upwards as she brought her lips round. Ryan's
mouth took hers, but it was a gentle exploration, as if
he wanted to know the taste, feel and substance of her.
Consequently it was more devastating to her soul than
the most erotic kiss. Disarmed by gentleness, Mickey
shivered sensually as the stroke of his tongue traced the
outline of her lips. He was making no other move to
touch her, and yet her breath caught in her throat and
her body flowered, making her ultra-sensitive to every
subtle nuance.

It wasn't until he raised his head what seemed like an
aeon later that the dim light showed her the blaze in his
blue eyes, and the tension in his face.

'Enough,' he gritted out, and she realised the strain
he was under to comfort and not seduce.

Emotion swelled inside her as she wondered how he
could give like that. She had felt she was undergoing the
sweetest torture, yet knowing it wasn't enough. It hadn't
come close to what she wanted—to touch and be
touched. While she had ached for more, he had been
denying himself. Yet strangely her self-indulgence didn't
make her feel ashamed. No, she knew she had to take
his gift and not hurt him more.

So she eased away from him, on to her back, meaning
to move back to her own blanket, but fate took a hand.
Her action brought his arm from round her, and his hand
came to rest on her breast. They both drew breath
raggedly, afraid to move. But there was no way to stop
her flesh responding, her nipple hardening and thrusting
up into his palm through the layers of shirt and vest.
Suddenly the air thickened around them.

'God, Mickey, it's *not* enough!' Ryan exclaimed in a
pained voice, and her stomach contracted.

'I know,' she moaned, and there was not a thing in
the world which could have stopped her then from

moving back into his arms, not even her own experience. She took a giant leap beyond that, and it was not even a memory.

With a groan, Ryan briefly closed his eyes before his head swooped down again, taking her lips in a deep, drugging kiss. With a helpless whimper of pleasure, Mickey parted her lips, senses rioting as he instantly accepted the invitation and embarked on an erotic plundering of her softness, urging her to join him, which she did boldly, shuddering at the waves of heat which surged to every quivering inch of her flesh.

When he moved his body against hers, she welcomed the solidity of his muscular thigh between her own. A pulse throbbed deep inside her, and was echoed by the thunderous beat of their two hearts. She wanted to be closer and closer, to be part of him, and the inevitability of their impassioned kisses could only thrill, not chill her.

Feverish fingers dealt with buttons and zips, then shirt and vests were gone, and there was only the stunning sensation of flesh on flesh. Neither felt the chill in the air as Ryan rubbed his hair-covered chest against the softness of her breasts. Mickey arched herself into that erotic caress, feeling her body ache for the touch of his hands, catching her breath on a cry as finally his hand closed on her turgid flesh, kneading it into a throbbing globe which he raised to his descending mouth.

All was delirium as his tongue lapped, flicked and teased her nipple before he drew her more deeply in, to suckle. Nearly sobbing, she raked his back with her nails, and knew a spear of delight as he arched and shuddered in response. When her hands plunged beneath the waistband of his jeans he moved against her, making her vitally aware of the strength of his arousal. Then with a groan he levered himself away from her, but her sigh of protest died when he bent to divest them both of their last remaining clothes.

Then he was back with her, gliding between her thighs, hands moulding her hips, lifting her legs to urge her to lock them around him. Mickey's head went back as she felt his manhood brushing the moist centre of her. She could hardly breathe as she held his slick body to her own glistening one. She wanted to tell him she couldn't bear to wait any longer, but somehow he knew, and he came into her, thrusting deeply. Everything was too white-hot to allow for control, even if either of them could have had any. Ryan's thrusts increased their pace, and she moved with him, holding on as an almost intolerable coil of tension grew and grew until there was nowhere to go but out over the edge as incredible pleasure exploded inside her. Seconds later Ryan joined her, his body convulsing as he groaned out her name.

Floating dazedly back to earth, Mickey felt Ryan drawing her into his arms and the protection of his warm body. She couldn't think, even though she knew she should. Her eyes felt weighted, and blackness hovered at the edges of her mind. She just had time to sense the blankets being pulled over her before sleep claimed her.

CHAPTER SEVEN

IT HAD been light for some time when Mickey stirred, and the first thing she became aware of was the rough texture of the blanket she was lying on. Then, of course, she was wide awake, for the only way she could feel that was if she had no clothes on—and the events of the night returned with a rush.

Her eyes flew open, and, aghast, she found herself staring up into Ryan's face. There was an expression in his eyes which she couldn't read, but his mouth curved gently. He looked rakishly charming, with a growth of beard on his cheeks, and Mickey felt sick. Oh, God, what had she done?

Gentle amusement danced across his face. 'Good morning.'

She closed her eyes briefly. What was he laughing at? The fact that she had caved in without a fight? When she looked at him again, he had sobered.

'What's the matter? Regretting it already?' he questioned, and his voice had hardened too.

Swallowing hard, Mickey looked away. 'Aren't you?' she challenged, looking round rather desperately for her clothes. She couldn't move until she had them.

Ryan's nostrils flared as he breathed in deeply, and slowly he shook his head. 'I wasn't. Last night certainly wasn't planned, but, hell, neither of us could help ourselves.'

Mickey winced as his words sank in. She already knew she couldn't help herself, knew what she was capable of when the dark side of her nature took over. Now all her efforts to fight it were rendered useless, because last night

117

had proved she had no self-control at all. All it took was
a handsome man with bewitching sex appeal to make
her...make her roll over and beg to be made love to!
Self-contempt echoed round and round in her brain,
scourging her.

Sick to her stomach, she sat up. Her clothes were scat-
tered around, mixed up with his, and, wincing, she
reached for her own, managing to pull on her vest before
Ryan sat up too. Immediately she wanted to run, but
there was nowhere to go in the cramped space they had
found to sleep in.

'Mickey?' Her name was a question as he touched her
shoulder, and the saying of it tore her apart inside, so
that she inexplicably felt raw and bleeding.

Confusion panicked her, and she uttered the first
words which entered her mind. 'Keep your hands off
me!'

Immediately his hand was withdrawn, only to close
on her chin and force her head round. There were storm
clouds threatening in his blue gaze. 'What the hell does
that mean?'

She had to force her lips together to stop them trembling before she spoke. 'Don't you think you did enough
touching last night?' she choked thickly, and was re-
warded with a lightning flash of anger in his eyes.

'Oh, no, sweetheart, that's not on. I didn't attack you
last night, Hanlon. You were with me all the way. In
fact, you damn near led the way!'

Mickey knew it was the truth, but it was the abrupt
return to the use of her surname which turned the screw,
reminding her just what he really thought of her. She
reacted blindly. 'That worked to your advantage, didn't
it? You got what you wanted without having to go to
too much trouble! Another conquest for the mighty Ryan
Douglas, and I made it so easy for you!' she charged,
feeling as if she was about to explode with emotions
which she didn't recognise. Her fists clenched on her

blanket as she forced herself not to look away from his growing anger. 'What a swell joke it must be for you to realise just how easy I was!'

Ryan's anger melted like snow in the spring, to be replaced by disbelief. 'Where are you coming from, Hanlon? No man with even half a brain would ever think you were easy! Easy? Compared to you, the Russian classics are a piece of cake!' he informed her with lashings of irony.

Mickey dropped her head, unable to take comfort from his statement. Reaching for her panties and jeans, she struggled into them in a state of deepening misery, knowing she had been blaming him for her own folly. He didn't know her failings, and how could she really blame him for taking advantage of them when they were offered? Now she had to retrieve the situation with as much dignity as she could.

'OK, so I'm not easy,' she revised flippantly, feeling his eyes on her, but refusing to look at him. 'I'm sure you've some other way of describing me now.'

Unseen, Ryan shot her the strangest look, compounded of so many nuances that it was impossible to identify them. 'Oh, I'd say you're dangerous, Hanlon. More dangerous than you know,' he decided thoughtfully.

Her green eyes flickered with shock. 'Dangerous? Don't be ridiculous!'

Ryan began reaching for his clothes. 'Perhaps you don't know yourself too well,' he suggested.

Mickey dragged her eyes away from his broad, tanned chest, and hid the colour which rose into her cheeks by shrugging into her shirt. 'I know myself quite well enough, thank you!' she snapped, scrambling to her feet and just avoiding cracking her head on the roof in her rush. Tossing the blanket aside, she jammed her feet into her boots, tied them, and went to thrust the door open.

It was a beautiful morning, the air crisp and clear. What was left of the mist was quickly evaporating. Mickey was just taking a good deep lungful of it when Ryan spoke.

'I'd be interested to know who it was who told you you were easy, Hanlon.'

A sledge-hammer landed in her chest, and she swivelled to stare at him. He hadn't moved, but sat looking at her with an animal watchfulness. What on earth had made him ask that? 'Nobody told me,' she answered huskily. Nobody, that was, except herself, and that was quite enough. 'I...' Whatever she might have said remained unspoken as she broke off and tilted her head. 'Listen!' Jumping down on to the float, she hastily scanned the sky to the north, her sharp eyes quickly picking up a welcome sight. 'It's Sid!'

'Good old Sid,' Ryan drawled as he came to the door and followed her pointing finger.

Mickey glanced at him sharply, relieved to see he had got his jeans on. 'Don't be sarcastic! He's come to help us.'

An eyebrow rose in a manner she knew she would never forget. 'Just in the nick of time, eh, Hanlon?' he continued softly, and she felt warmth climb into her cheeks as she looked away, refusing to answer.

Jumping on to the beach, Mickey ran along to where Sid was now bringing his float plane down to land on the water. She was honest enough to know there was relief in the wave she sent him, for his arrival meant she would no longer be alone with Ryan. Biting her lip, she glanced back at Amelia. Ryan had remained where he was. Framed in the doorway, feet and torso bare, he looked so powerfully, potently male, and he attracted her like a magnet. She longed to go back, and knew the pull of the dark side had already started. But perhaps, just perhaps, if she didn't let her passions overcome her again, there might be a chance to paper over the cracks in her defences.

She refused to analyse the tiny ache under her ribs as she watched the aircraft come to rest before her. Ready to catch the mooring rope, she was stunned to see a complete stranger climb out of the door, and nimbly navigate the float. Dropping down beside her, he proceeded to make the rope fast. There was time for her to take in the fact that he was young, with a shock of ginger hair, and wore glasses which did nothing for his rather homely face, before she received her next shock.

'Mickey!'

With a gasp, she turned round to see Leah jumping down, and only managed to register the beautiful smile she wore before her sister was flinging herself into her arms. Mickey returned the hug automatically, realising she had almost forgotten the reason she was out here. That sobered her instantly, and she quickly put the young woman at arm's length.

'Leah, where on earth have you been?' she demanded, examining her sister's face minutely for signs of distress, but seeing only a shining happiness.

Leah laughed. 'Everywhere! Isn't it wonderful?' With a smooth action she freed herself and held out her hand, smiling over Mickey's shoulder. 'Peter, come and meet my sister.' When he obediently took her hand, Leah clung to his arm. 'Darling, this is Mickey.'

Mickey found herself staring dumbfounded at the smiling couple. 'This is Peter?' she muttered, staggered by the knowledge that the man she had pictured in her mind as some glowing, bronzed, handsome playboy was anything but, and indeed, didn't look as if he would be offended if you called him studious!

And Leah, the normal calm, dignified, intense Leah, was almost jumping with excitement. 'Yes. Peter Douglas, my husband.'

Mickey couldn't have said anything, and didn't need too.

'Your what?' an inimical voice demanded from behind them, and they all turned as one to discover Ryan had approached unheard. Fully dressed, he stood before them, hands on hips, glowering.

To give him credit, Peter was not cowed. Just as if they were meeting on a city street, he held out his hand. 'Hi, Ryan. We came as soon as Sophie passed on Mickey's message.'

It was the first time Mickey had ever seen the mighty Ryan Douglas taken aback, and she had trouble holding back a laugh. He sent her a long, hard look, but before he could speak Leah was holding out her hand, her smile gently welcoming.

'Hello, Mr Douglas. I've heard so much about you from Peter that I feel I know you already.'

Mickey watched with interest as Ryan was forced, out of good manners, to shake hands with the errant couple. However, he was not to be side-tracked for long.

'Did you say *Mickey's* message?' he demanded abruptly.

Peter looked surprised. 'Yes. Didn't you know?'

Ryan's face wore a grim smile. 'For some reason Mickey chose not to tell me. Why don't you do the honours?' he suggested, sending her a look which promised he'd get to her later.

Peter cleared his throat, clearly sensing undercurrents here. 'Apparently she rang Sophie at a friend's house and insisted she radio in to us to tell me about Bobby. By the way, I rang home when we got in last night. They think he might be coming out of it. I said we'd be home tomorrow.'

His uncle nodded. 'Well, that's good news anyway,' Ryan said with obvious relief. Then he crossed his arms and regarded his nephew sardonically. 'However, don't run away with the idea that you've smoothed everything over. You still have a hell of a lot of explaining to do, the pair of you. You can start with your letter.'

The young couple exchanged rueful looks, and then it was Leah who answered. 'You see, Peter felt so badly about not keeping in touch that he had to send it, even though he knew it would probably bring you here.'

Ryan was not about to receive short change. 'Having made sure it would already be too late.'

Leah's chin went up in a way Mickey could only admire. 'Yes. You would only have tried to stop us, and we're old enough to make our own decisions.'

'I knew what you'd think, Ryan, after I made such a fool of myself not long ago, but this is different,' Peter insisted. 'I know what I want now: to be the best doctor I can be, and have Leah as my wife. And she hasn't married me for my money either.'

'No, indeed.' Leah instantly took up the reins, her expression serious. 'I can understand your worrying, but I have more than enough money of my own. Surely Mickey told you that?' Here she looked at her sister for support, and Mickey felt compelled to give it, to a point.

'I did, but he wasn't prepared to believe me,' she agreed. 'Though that didn't hurt me nearly so much as the fact that you didn't tell me about Peter yourself.'

Leah was patently contrite, but just as obviously not sorry. 'Oh, Mickey, I would have loved to tell you. I wanted to, but how could I? I love Peter, but you don't believe in love. You'd have done your best to split us up, simply because someone hurt you in the past. But Mickey, Peter isn't going to treat me like that. I'm sorry if that hurt you, but I wasn't prepared to give Peter up for you or anyone. Which is why we went to Grandmother Sophie, and she told us we must do what we felt was right for both of us.'

Peter slipped an arm about her shoulder, and hugged her. 'Which we did. We got married and had a short honeymoon sailing around the islands. We were already on our way back to tell you what we had done when the message about Bobby reached us. We intend to make arrangements for Leah to transfer to my university, so we can set up house together while we carry on with our medical careers.'

Mickey watched them with a hollow feeling in her stomach, seeing their happiness and knowing Leah was right. She would have tried to make her sister see things the way she herself did, and that would have been wrong. Peter was not another Jean-Luc. He was a sensible, dedicated young man, who had made one mistake, a mistake he had learned from, so he had recognised the goodness in Leah. They would be happy together. They were soul mates. Envy gnawed away at her insides, and she watched as they presented a united front while Peter talked with his uncle.

Feeling unable to watch any more, and knowing that for the moment she had been forgotten, Mickey took the opportunity to slip away. She needed to think, and kept on walking along the beach until a fallen tree blocked her path. Stopping, she rested against it, only then hearing the crunch of footsteps which told she had been followed after all. Bracing herself to see Ryan, she turned to find it was Leah hovering a little way away, concern dimming the glow in her eyes.

'I'm sorry, Mickey,' she apologised contritely. 'The truth is I couldn't think of any other way.'

Mickey winced. 'I've not been much of a sister, have I?'

Leah took a hasty step closer. 'Oh, no, it wasn't that! You see, when I told Dad how odd I thought it that you never dated, he told me you had had an unhappy affair. Of course I understood then, but I was unhappy for you. I thought you were bound to get over it one day, but you never did. Then I met Peter. The first thing I wanted to do was tell you, but he'd also told me about his in-volvement with another woman not long ago. It didn't make him look good, and I knew that, with the best will in the world, your... biased... outlook would see everything for the worst. You've cut men out of your life so determinedly that I was afraid you'd try to make me do the same!'

Mickey was aghast, more so because of the truth of it. 'Oh, Leah!'

'I couldn't take the chance, so we planned this, because Peter felt exactly the same about his uncle. I see now we were wrong; we should have trusted. Now I've hurt you terribly, haven't I?' she said gruffly, on the verge of tears.

Unable to bear seeing her sister unhappy, Mickey hastily put her arms round her. 'No. Not really. You were right, darling, and I was wrong. I could have hurt you more because of my own... disappointments. I had no idea you knew anything. What a cold, hard woman I must seem! I'm so sorry that I forced you to act in a way you normally never would have. You have every right to be happy with the man of your choice.' Here she pulled away to grin faintly. 'Though I have to admit Peter is nothing like I imagined him.'

Leah grinned back. 'I know he isn't some musclebound Romeo, but I love him. He'll be good for me. I only wish you could find someone to make you happy too, Mickey. Someone like Ryan,' she ventured in all seriousness.

Mickey felt a shock-wave run through her at the suggestion, and forced a laugh through a tight throat. 'Ryan? Don't be silly! And don't worry about me. I've never been happier since I came here to find Father, and found you too, of course.' Thankfully Leah didn't follow up her suggestion.

'But you'll be all alone when I'm gone.'

Now Mickey produced a laugh which wasn't forced. 'Don't think you've seen the last of me. I'll probably be

descending on you so often, you'll get sick of the sight
of me.'

'Never! You'll always be welcome,' Leah protested,
and they hugged each other one more time.

'Is it safe to join you?' a voice asked from behind
them, and they turned.

Peter was standing a short way away, not uncertain,
but waiting for an invitation. He raised an eyebrow at
his wife, and, when he received a nod, unleashed a quite
devastating smile on Mickey, which showed the young
man had hidden depths. She could see there was no side
to him and, with the generosity of her old self, held out
her hand and drew him forward to kiss his cheek.

'Welcome to the family, Peter. Perhaps this wasn't the
best beginning, but I hope that in future you will both
think you can come to me if you need any help,' she
offered generously.

Peter let out his breath in relief. 'Leah said you'd come
round. I had quite a talk with Ryan too. He tore me off
a strip about running off that way, but then he wished
us both happy, so everything has turned out for the best
after all.'

It was hardly surprising that that seemed to cheer the
young couple immensely.

Leah held out her hands to both of them. 'Shall we
go back? Poor old Amelia needs all the attention now.'

'Not so much of the old,' Mickey protested. 'She gets
us where we want to go...mostly,' she added with a grin,
and they were all laughing as they walked back.

They discovered Ryan helping Sid work on the engine.
Mickey found herself staring at Ryan's back while it
slowly dawned her that, with the return of the runaways, there was nothing to keep him here. It was as if
a chasm suddenly opened up at her feet, a kind of
yawning despair which she quickly had to tell herself
was ridiculous. She wanted him gone. He had been
nothing but trouble since the moment he arrived. So why,

then, was it that, with his departure imminent, she found she wanted to tell him not to go? The answer came with the increased beat of her heart as he moved and the muscles of his back rippled beneath his shirt. Memories of how his skin had felt and tasted assailed her, and she craved more, just as she had despaired she would, if ever she dropped her guard. Which was why she must never say the words, for even if the longing made her ache now it would fade with his going, just as her passion had for Jean-Luc.

'If it isn't too much bother, Hanlon, perhaps you'd care to try the engine.'

Ryan's sarcastic comment drew her out of her introspection with a jolt. Lord, but he was obnoxious! If they'd been alone she would have fired off a salvo to cut him down to size, but, as he was very much aware, they were not alone, so she could only seethe up at his mocking figure.

'How could I refuse such a gallantly phrased request?' she replied sweetly as she climbed aboard. Yet she couldn't resist a sibilant aside as she passed him. 'You can't know how I'm looking forward to you disappearing over the horizon!'

That ridiculous eyebrow lifted again. 'You won't miss me?'

Her heart knocked, but she resolutely ignored it. 'As I'd miss a burst appendix!' was her riposte as she went in and took her seat, making preparations to start the engine.

When it fired first time and then took on a steady drone, she really should have been cheering, but it wasn't in her. She just felt incredibly tired.

'Cheer up, Hanlon, or you'll be having me thinking you lied just now,' Ryan chivvied her through the open flap of the window. 'I'll miss you, you know, although I can't decide whether that's for the cutting edge of your

tongue, or the soft curves of your body which you nestled
so tightly against mine last night.'

Mickey gaped at him in angry dismay, very much
aware that not only had Sid heard every word, but Leah
and Peter, too. Hot colour stormed up her neck into her
cheeks. 'I could kill you for that!' she gritted through
her teeth, skating her eyes away from her sister's surprised look, only to encounter Peter's knowing one.

Obligingly, Ryan dropped his voice to a whisper. 'All's
fair in love and war.'

The suddenness of his return to the attack was painful,
but she should have guessed he wouldn't let her get away
with saying nothing about the message she had sent.
'You're a sore loser, Ryan,' she retorted scathingly.
'Maybe next time you won't be so quick to jump to
conclusions.'

That brought an intentness to his eyes which held her
transfixed. 'Unless, of course, they're ones you want me
to jump to, eh, Hanlon? Now, if you'll switch off again,
we can finish up and get out of here,' he concluded, and
disappeared without giving her a chance to answer.

Mickey did as she was told, feeling all the while that
she had just lost a pound and found a penny. What had
he meant by that remark? It was impossible to tell from
his face. Nor was there much opportunity for thought,
for in what seemed like no time at all the faulty part had
been replaced and they were all standing on the beach
again.

Much to her dismay, Ryan appeared to have taken
charge. 'We should be OK now, Sid, so why don't you
take our two love-birds back to Prince Rupert? Hanlon
and I will follow once I've had a chance to wash up.'

'That OK with you, Mickey?' Sid checked with her,
and there was little she could say, because to say, Don't
leave without me, would be childish in the extreme.

Caught, she shrugged. 'Sure. We won't be far behind
you in any case,' she added for good measure.

'And don't make any plans for tonight, because you're all invited to Sophie's for supper. She wants to make amends, and it will be the only opportunity, as Peter's flight leaves in the small hours,' Leah put in swiftly, before giving in to her husband's urging to get in the plane.

There was nothing left for Mickey to do then but wave as the three of them took off again. But once the float plane had become nothing more than a speck she was very much aware that she was once more alone with Ryan. She turned to face him, and he was watching her with a strange look in his eye.

'Why didn't you tell me about the message, Hanlon?' he demanded immediately, just as she had known he would.

She shrugged offhandedly. 'Because Sophie is an old lady, despite how she seems to you. I didn't want you rushing out there and harassing her. I knew she'd act quickly once she knew the truth, and that Peter's return would be answer enough.'

Ryan made to run his hand through his hair, then thought better of it when he saw it was oil-smeared. 'OK, I guess I can accept that, but that doesn't explain why you claimed yesterday you would take me to my nephew for a quarter of a million dollars, when you already knew he must be on his way back to Prince Rupert. What was the point of that, Hanlon?'

Mickey licked her lips nervously. The truth was out of the question, even though the events of the night had negated the reasons for the lie. 'You seemed to expect it of me,' she told him shortly. 'You knew I needed money, and I was sick to death of your taunts about Leah. I decided to get some of my own back.'

One eyebrow rose lazily. 'Is that what it was? Then my thinking you said it to make me back off, once you saw your taunt about mixing me up with your fiancé had failed, is wrong?'

All her breath seemed to leave her lungs with a whoosh at the accuracy of his taunt. 'Totally wrong,' she agreed faintly.

He pursed his lips thoughtfully. 'And you weren't using your words like weapons again?'

Her legs felt weak. 'Absolutely not,' she denied, wishing she could sound more convincing, yet knowing she might easily fall foul of overkill.

'Hmm.'

Mickey didn't like the sound of that at all, and, desperately needing to do something to break what felt like a straitjacket of tension, she headed for Amelia.

'I'll get you the soap. I keep some with a towel for times like these,' she babbled as she excused herself, and tried not to think that to him she must look as if she was scuttling away. When she returned, Ryan had already removed his shirt, and she had to swallow hard as she handed him the soap.

She had intended to move away, but as he knelt beside the water and began to lather his arms and face she found she was rooted to the spot. The breadth of his chest was tantalising, with its sprinkling of silky dark hair. As he moved, muscles rippled in his back, and she had an almost overwhelming compulsion to run her hands over the tanned planes.

'Nothing's stopping you, Hanlon,' Ryan murmured softly, and she was shocked to discover he was regarding her over his shoulder, his eyes darkened by the same turbulent memories as were running through her own mind.

Heat scorched her face as she realised how transparent her emotions were to him. With a stifled moan of shame she turned to flee, but not fast enough. His hand shot out, catching her ankle, tripping her so that she tumbled to the ground. He was over her in a second, his large frame pinning her down. Mickey tried to hold him off, but the hands she pressed against his shoulders turned traitor and clung to his hot skin instead.

'You can touch me as much as you like,' Ryan invited huskily, and her eyes dropped to his chest as her hands obeyed him. She found it so hard to breathe, and lost what breath she had when her hand hovered over his heart and felt the wild thudding it made. She looked up at once, and met his descending head.

She was lost in seconds. There was no thought in her to avoid his kiss. She wanted it with something near to desperation. It was like last night all over again, all pure heat and sensation, wiping everything from her mind as she returned kiss for kiss, erotic caress for erotic caress. She didn't want to be passive. She wanted to touch him as he was touching her, to taunt and tease him, hold and possess him.

He rolled over, taking her with him, so that she lay spread-eagled on top of him, her thighs framing his. His teeth bit at her lips, then his tongue sought the erotic duel of hers again, and she matched him, shivering as his hands pulled her shirt from her jeans and burrowed their way beneath to sear her skin, tracing the line of her spine before trailing round to cup her breasts and encircle her turgid nipples with his thumbs.

Mickey gasped aloud, tearing her mouth free to drag in air, and it was only then, as the chill breeze struck her fevered flesh, that it came to her what she was doing, what she was allowing. With a cry she thrust away, only to find she was still sitting astride him in the most intimate way. Yet before she could move, Ryan jack-knifed upwards, so that they were once more chest to chest.

There was hectic colour in his cheeks, and a wildness in his eyes. 'Oh, no, you don't, Hanlon. You don't run away now, leaving me aching for you!' he growled, catching her wrists.

Mickey struggled for freedom. 'I don't want this!' she cried, voice breaking.

'The hell you say! Don't take me for a fool, Hanlon; you want me as much now as you did last night.'

She shuddered and forced herself to go still. It took an effort, but her voice came out cold and steady. 'Maybe so, but last night was a mistake I don't intend to make again!' she insisted. 'Now let me go.'

Ryan looked stunned. 'How can you turn your back so easily on what we shared?'

Mickey's lashes fluttered down. It wasn't easy at all. 'Because I don't want you in my life. I didn't plan for you to come along and complicate things!' she exclaimed.

He frowned. 'Because of Jack? Hell, engagements are made to be broken!'

Unwittingly he had given her the opening, and she took it gratefully. 'I don't want to lose Jack. Certainly not for the doubtful pleasure of a brief fling with you!'

Blue eyes grew narrow and flinty, and abruptly he thrust her away and got stiffly to his feet. 'You'd better get up. If we stay here much longer I may be tempted to do something I'll come to regret. But take heed, sweetheart; you'd better get control of those wild passions of yours. It's a dangerous game you're playing. Next time I might not be able to stop.'

Mickey clambered inelegantly to her feet, not daring to look at him, wishing the ground would open and swallow her up. 'There won't be a next time,' she declared hoarsely, and hurried back to the plane as fast as her still trembling legs could carry her. She'd make good and sure there was never a next time, because she was dreadfully afraid that she wouldn't be able to stop either.

Within fifteen minutes they were airborne again, heading back home. For the first half-hour not a word was spoken to break the chilly silence. Mickey grew more and more subdued, hating the atmosphere which had grown between them. Just when she thought she'd reached screaming point, Ryan spoke.

'Does Jack know about your unhappy love-affair?' he asked baldly, making her gasp aloud, a reaction which drew cold eyes to her face.

She had to clear her throat before answering, while her mind wondered just where this was heading. 'Jack knows everything.'

'So you're going to tell him about me—us?' Ryan queried, not masking his disbelief.

Mickey drew a steadying breath. 'There is no us, just a one-night stand.'

'He's not the forgiving sort, then?' he persisted.

For a moment she felt a hysterical desire to laugh at the absurdity of finding herself defending a mythical man. 'Jack is a wonderful person.'

His smile was mocking. 'If he's that wonderful, why me at all? Apparently in the passion stakes he's something of a non-starter.'

Mickey's teeth snapped together angrily. 'I refuse to discuss my relationship with Jack. It's none of your business.'

Ryan laughed at that. 'The poor sap isn't married to you yet, and already he's being cuckolded. That doesn't bode well for your marriage,' he declared contemptuously, and she paled.

'I think you've said quite enough!'

'You should let him go, Hanlon. You'll only make him miserable, and it's clear he'll never satisfy you,' Ryan went on bluntly.

She should have felt angry with him for that, but it only made her depressed. 'Thanks for the vote of confidence!'

His mouth twisted nastily. 'Meaning you won't give him up. What are you trying to do—make Jack pay for what that other man did to you? That's warped thinking, Hanlon. The only way to get on with your life is to let him go too.'

Of all the things he said, that was the one she was least able to follow. 'I have no intention of ever forgetting Jean-Luc!'

She had made him angry again. She could hear it in his voice, but for the life of her she didn't know why, for she was nothing to him.

'Why? What did he ever do for you except apparently ruin your life?'

Now she couldn't help but look at him. 'And what have you ever done for me, except cause trouble?' she virtually shouted at him, just like a fishwife.

Ryan's face became shuttered. 'According to Sophie, I brought you to life again. Even Jack failed to do that,' he retorted, finding the mark.

For an instant her face broke up. 'Then I wish to God you'd left me as you found me!'

A muscle jerked in his jaw. 'You don't mean that,' he contradicted tautly.

Her mouth pressed together tightly. 'I do!'

The laugh he gave was grim. 'Then you're more of a fool than I thought!' he said, and turned his shoulder on her, leaving a silence so cold that it seeped into her bones.

Mickey finished the rest of the journey on automatic pilot, doing all the right things, although ever afterwards she could not recall an inch of the distance they covered. Only when she taxied in to the landing-stage did she really realise where she was, and that all her muscles felt stiff, as if she had been holding herself rigid for hours. As she switched off, Sid came out to tie the mooring rope, and she was finally forced to look at her silent companion.

'I'll send my bill to your office, shall I?' she queried, wishing she wasn't always so vitally aware of the man beside her.

His lips curled. 'Don't want to take the risk of seeing me in person to receive payment?'

'I rather thought you wouldn't want to see me,' she retorted, stung.

Ryan smiled. 'I've nothing against seeing you, Hanlon. After all, we're distantly related now, so we'll be seeing quite a lot of each other.'

That hadn't occurred to her, and she took in the consequences of it in a daze. 'So you'll be at Sophie's tonight?'

'Where else?' he taunted, and Mickey decided she couldn't stand it another second. But as she made to get up and leave, Ryan's hand came out to grasp her arm and stop her. Her eyes shot to his in alarm, and saw his flicker. 'Not so fast, Hanlon. There's one last thing to be settled between us,' he growled, and pulled her down on to his lap, clasping her tightly to his chest whilst his mouth swooped on hers.

It was a kiss which, from the very beginning, stirred her to the depths of her being, calling forth a tumultuous passion which set her alight. Within seconds there was a fever raging in her blood, making demands which she had to respond to. To fight was impossible, to remain passive unthinkable. She *had* to return his kiss and unleash the wild thing that was their mutual passion. With a soft cry she freed one arm and flung it round his neck, shuddering out her pleasure as his hand burrowed beneath her shirt, seeking her flesh, branding it as he found and claimed the surging peak of her breast. At the mercy of a passion she couldn't control, Mickey could only arch and press herself against him as he cupped her swollen flesh, sending wave after wave of delirium down through her to start up that ache of need between her thighs.

Then, as suddenly as she had been captured, she was released and thrust back into her own seat, left to stare up at him while her heart thudded wildly and she gasped at each laboured breath. In contrast, Ryan's face was closed and unreadable.

'I don't think I'll be at Sophie's tonight after all. Make my excuses. I'm sure you'll be only too happy to think of something appropriate. Goodbye, Hanlon, it's been an education!' Ryan dismissed scathingly, and left her without a backward glance.

CHAPTER EIGHT

IT WAS a week later, to the day, after their acrimonious parting that Mickey discovered a letter from her mother. It had lain hidden among the mail she had left unopened on the kitchen table when she went to work that morning. She *had* been going through the motions of making supper, but all thought of eating vanished at once, as it had had a tendency to do ever since Ryan had left. Usually she had sense enough to eat something, but this missive put paid to that. She delayed opening it while she made herself a pot of tea. Her hand shook as she poured it out, but that didn't surprise her. She was barely sleeping and hardly eating, and her nerves were so shot that she flared up at the least little thing.

Even the phlegmatic Sid was threatening to leave. Just this morning he had told her either to go after Ryan or stop feeling sorry for herself. She had been so shocked that she had simply stared at him, and Sid had sighed and relented.

'Mickey, if you want that fella, you gotta let him know it. He ain't a mind-reader. Nobody is. I'm telling you, if you let him get away, you'll be sorry,' he had told her gruffly.

She was sorry already, had been virtually from the moment the float plane had stopped rocking after Ryan stepped off it. But what kind of woman would it make her if she ran after a man simply because overnight she had developed an addiction for his brand of loving? Wasn't that the very thing she had sworn not to do, because it was another step on a road she didn't want to travel?

137

And yet she wanted Ryan. Missed him with an ache which wouldn't go away. Longed to have him hold her, touch her. Longed, even, for the sound of his voice. Feeling as she did, it would be so easy to feed the fire burning inside her, but it would burn out, as all fires did, leaving her...where? To end up like her mother? Going from affair to affair in an endless search for new thrills? It made nausea rise in her throat. Which was why she felt as if she was being torn apart, and it was slowly but surely sapping the life out of her.

Sid meant well, but he was thinking in terms of marriage, when an affair was all it would ever be. Ryan was looking for the love of his life, and she didn't need him to tell her she wasn't that. She was just a brief diversion along the way. In fact he had never actually said he wanted an affair with her, although he had wanted her. So even if she did make the fateful decision to go after him, she had no expectation of him welcoming her back into his life. Their relationship had not been a happy one, and their parting still made her wince.

She hadn't seen him since that morning. He hadn't been at Sophie's, and, although nobody had blamed her for his absence, Mickey still felt responsible. Her actions had kept him away, and that hadn't been right, especially when he had had to leave next day with Peter. But even that didn't explain why she should feel so bereft, or why she had found herself driving past the hotel he had stayed in like some lovesick idiot.

She kept telling herself she should be relieved he was gone, but she only felt numb. She'd been numb ever since.

Lacing her tea with sugar, Mickey sat down and reluctantly opened the letter. A card fell out, and she found herself staring blankly at a wedding invitation. She was too hardened to the sight to be shocked by it, although it did surprise her to realise her mother was marrying again after all these years. The shock came in the letter itself.

> But darling, you must come, and bring your fiancé with you. After all, it's about time he met your mother. Shouldn't you be married by now, anyway? Surely two years is long enough to get to know anybody, darling! I won't accept any excuses this time, and if you don't come I'll begin to think you're ashamed of me. So I'll expect you both on the eighteenth.

Mickey stared at the words which caught her out in a lie. It had seemed so simple, two years ago, to invent a fiancé to stop her mother from worrying, and possibly interfering in her life. Many times Tanita had declared a wish to meet this mythical man, but Mickey had been able to fob her off with reasonable excuses. This time, though, her mother had pre-empted her. Not to turn up would be unthinkable, because she wasn't ashamed of her mother, and never had been.

Mickey dropped her head in her hands and laughed, laughed until she was on the verge of tears. Her world, which she had so recently thought so secure, was tumbling down around her. Self-knowledge was hard won, but she recognised something now. She had lied to everybody, but more importantly to herself, and a life built of such flimsy material was doomed to collapse. She had been fairly and squarely hoist by her own petard, and there was nothing for it but to turn up at the wedding and admit she didn't have a fiancé, and never had had.

Ten days later Mickey boarded her flight, having left Sid in temporary charge of the business. She felt exhausted, for not only had she had to prepare for her own trip, but help make the arrangements for Leah's move east to join Peter. To cap it all, her sister had insisted on taking her shopping, with the result that she now possessed several good outfits.

She was wearing one now, an uncrushable suit of royal blue, which the assistant had assured her would be perfect for travelling in. Mickey had to admit it fitted well and it looked good, suiting her perfectly, and, although she would have preferred to travel in trousers, her mother would be meeting the plane and would expect to see her daughter properly dressed.

It was a long flight, with several stops, and she had lost interest in the changing faces of the passengers by the time they reached Toronto. She didn't leave her seat, choosing to read a magazine, and barely looked up when someone else took the vacant space beside her. Out of the corner of her eye she saw a pair of male legs stretch out, and automatically shifted away from them, an action which unfortunately dragged the knee-length skirt up her thighs.

'So you do possess legs. I was beginning to wonder. I'd even fantasised about them. Now I can see they were worth the wait,' a mocking voice declared, and Mickey's heart gave an almighty leap as she shot round.

'Ryan?' Shock mingled with disbelief and an exhilarating wave of pleasure. 'What are you doing here?' Even to her own ears her voice sounded breathless.

'I distinctly remember telling you I would be going to Europe.'

She really shouldn't have imagined he had come after her, or felt so disappointed to realise he hadn't, especially after the way they had parted, but she did, and it was hard to keep the evidence off her face. 'Oh, yes, I remember. You said you were going to Greece.'

He smiled sardonically. 'It's gratifying to know you were paying attention, Hanlon. I did say that, but as there is no specific deadline I decided to take a detour. Where are you off to?'

Still in a state of shock, she had no chance to dissemble. 'Nice. My mother's getting married . . . again,' she volunteered wryly, and he easily picked up the tone.

'Don't you like him?'

Mickey shrugged. 'I've never met him, but I expect I shall like him. I've liked all the others,' she admitted offhandedly, and Ryan frowned.

'Others? This isn't her second marriage, then?' he queried, finally making her remember he had no idea who her mother was.

In the circumstances, she found it a relief to remain incognito. This time there would be no sly looks, or unspoken comparisons. 'No. You could call my mother an incurable romantic. She always thinks this is the big one, and never believes it can go wrong. A case of the triumph of hope over experience.'

Ryan watched her curiously. 'That's a very cynical remark. You don't approve?'

Mickey hadn't meant to give that impression at all. Her aim had been to make Tanita sound fairly ordinary, not at all the person her daughter knew her to be. She quickly shook her head. 'Believe me, I'm happy for her if it makes her happy.'

'But you don't think she will be?' he questioned astutely.

'Not at all. She's always happy...in the beginning. They just never last,' Mickey added wearily.

'At least she's not afraid to put it to the test,' Ryan went on smoothly.

'Meaning I am?' she challenged swiftly, realising rather too late her shock at seeing him had led her into a good many disclosures which she never should have made.

In reply Ryan picked up her left hand, isolating her bare marriage finger. 'You're not married.'

His touch sent an electric charge up her arm and raised the colour in her cheeks. And because she was tempted to close her hand around his, she quickly pulled away. 'No, but I am engaged.'

'Ah, yes, Jack. You've been engaged to him...what...two years now?' he queried thoughtfully, and for no accountable reason a shiver of alarm ran up her spine.

She narrowed her green eyes warningly. 'Yes, about that.'

'I didn't think I was wrong, so would you care to explain how neither Leah nor Sophie know anything about it?' Ryan asked conversationally, crossing his legs in a carelessly relaxed way.

Mickey was glad she was sitting down. 'What?'

'I said——' he began obligingly, but she cut him off.

'I know what you said. How could you have spoken to them about him?'

He raised both eyebrows. 'I assumed, their being close family, they would have known everything. You can imagine my surprise when they knew nothing. I came to the conclusion that either you didn't introduce him to them because you were either ashamed of them, or him, or that he didn't exist at all. Having got to know you fairly well, I plumped for the latter. Jack is a figment of your imagination, invented purely to keep me at arm's length.'

Mickey raised a faintly trembling hand to her forehead and rubbed at the dull ache that was forming. She had always been afraid of Ryan's astuteness, and now she knew she had been wise to be. A denial would gain her nothing now. 'If he was, he failed!' she declared bitterly, lowering her hand and doubling it into a fist.

Seeing it, Ryan attempted to pick up her hand, but she jerked it away. 'So, despite the clothes, you're still the same old "don't touch" Hanlon.'

She hated his mockery and flashed him a look of dislike. 'Did you think I would change just because you had me once?'

At once his eyes chilled. 'Vulgarity doesn't suit you, Hanlon. There was nothing tawdry about our lovemaking.'

Mickey flushed as vivid pictures swept through her mind, closely followed by a feeling of despair. Why was it that, when she had missed him so, it was anger he aroused in her now they had met again? This constant emotional see-sawing was doing her no good. There had to be an end to it one way or the other, and soon.

'There was nothing special about it either!' she said waspishly.

He looked amused. 'Speak for yourself. I have my own memories,' he advised provokingly, causing her chin to drop. However, before she could form a reply, he ran his eye over her in lazy inspection. 'You've been hiding your light under a bushel, Hanlon. The more I see, the more I have to wonder why you've been hiding that incredibly sexy body under those clothes you wear.'

Mickey's mouth twisted sourly. He could be so damned aggravating! 'To stop precisely that sort of comment!'

There was a curious quality to his smile. 'To say you have a sexy body is a fact, not a come-on. The truth of the matter is, Hanlon, that you'd look sexy in anything. Didn't you know that? Did you imagine people wouldn't notice? You are who and what you are in spite of the clothes you choose to wear,' he pronounced, never once taking his eyes from her face.

It was a fact which had been drilled home to her these last few dreadful weeks. 'I'm fully aware of that.'

'So the clothes aren't so much a disguise as a penance?'

She managed to hold back a gasp, but it was frightening the way he managed to cut through everything to the nitty-gritty. Somehow she had to counter-attack, or her silence would be tantamount to an admission. 'You're wrong. I don't see myself as some sort of saint.'

'I'm more inclined to the idea you see yourself as a sinner. Why? Because you had a love-affair which went wrong? It's hardly unique, Hanlon. It happens to the best of us. We're all human, and make mistakes.'

Lord, if he kept chipping away at her already depleted defences they'd crumble like a house of cards. 'Oh, please, if I want to listen to a sermon I go to church!' she declared sarcastically, hoping to head him off, but he wasn't to be moved so easily.

Ryan smiled grimly and shook his head. 'It won't wash, sweetheart.'

'What won't?'

'Trying to make me angry. I've been doing a lot of thinking these past few weeks, and I realised that when you make me angry I stop thinking. But when I've cooled down I see things much more clearly. So, you see, I'm on to you now.'

She very much feared he was, but couldn't understand why he should keep on and on at her. After all, he might want her physically, but that was all. What did he care what had happened or would happen to her? She felt threatened, and wanted to be left alone. Sarcasm hadn't worked; now she chose amusement.

'The only thing you're on to is a black eye,' she charged, managing to laugh. 'Of course I'm human, and make mistakes, but I happen to think there are some mistakes which shouldn't be repeated,' she added reasonably.

Characteristically, Ryan ignored the major part of her statement and went for the specifics. 'And what was your mistake?'

'Obviously thinking I was entitled to some privacy!' she snapped, irritated to the point of feeling her hands itch.

To her surprise, Ryan eyed her broodingly for a second or two, then shrugged and made himself more comfortable in his seat. Relieved, Mickey was just on the point of exhaling a shaky breath when he spoke as if he were discussing the weather.

'I still mean to find out.'

Her heart jumped, and she turned her head to stare at him, feeling besieged. 'Why?' she demanded hoarsely.

Ryan didn't look at her; in fact he closed his eyes. 'Would you believe, because I've fallen in love with you and want to marry you?'

That really hurt. To have him making fun of her brought a pain to the region of her heart that she had never expected. 'Frankly, no. I'm the last person you'd fall in love with, and we both know it.'

'Stranger things have happened.'

Mickey gasped. 'That wouldn't be strange, it would be insane.'

He laughed wryly. 'I couldn't argue with that,' he agreed, and said no more.

Mickey was left knowing he had been toying with her. It hurt all the more because she hadn't deserved it, and also it had been an action unworthy of him. She turned her gaze to the window. Why had he done it? To pay her back for refusing to give up her secrets? It was unfair. As unfair as the fates which had contrived to put him on this flight, dooming her to spend hours in his company, when what she really needed was to put him out of her mind.

So why, then, on hearing the steady sound of his breathing which signified he had fallen asleep, did she immediately turn and watch him? She told herself she was all kinds of a fool even as her eyes began to catalogue every detail of his face. She experienced a tiny shock to realise that, despite his state of relaxation, he looked tired. Almost as if he, like her, had been finding it hard to sleep. At which point her heart warmed to the knowledge that within half an hour of meeting her he had fallen into a deep sleep.

The absurdity of attributing that to her presence had her biting her lip. Lord, but she was having the craziest thoughts! He was tired, that was all, and the steady drone of the aircraft had simply sent him to sleep. Yet even that logic wouldn't dispel the warmth inside her. Instead she hugged it to her as she, in her turn, closed her eyes.

Hours later she stirred and opened her eyes. The first thing she saw was the outline of a distinctly masculine jaw. Then, as her other senses resurfaced, she breathed in a scent which she would have known anywhere. It intoxicated her, and she knew she would never tire of it. Her lips curved sensually. She'd bottle it, and call it 'Essence of Ryan', and every time she opened it she could imagine he was there with her.

At which point whimsy vanished as reality reminded her he *was* there, and that at some point during her sleep her head had dropped to his shoulder and remained there. Jerking upwards, her head connected with his chin and drew forth a soft expletive, and she experienced a tiny thrill as she realised that while her head had rested on his shoulder his head had been cushioned against her hair. The intimacy brought a warm flush to the whole of her body.

'Sorry,' she apologised huskily, and glanced up to find herself looking into sleepy blue eyes which warmed at the sight of her confusion.

'When you hurt someone, you're supposed to kiss them better,' he breathed, and she was about to correct him when his lips landed softly on hers and the thought flew from her mind.

The kiss was gentle, undemanding, a soft savouring of her which sent a tingle across her receptive nerves. It was impossible not to respond with butterfly movements of her own lips, and she wanted to cry out a protest when, after too brief a time, he raised his head again.

'Hmm, nice. I could get used to that,' he murmured, tracing a finger across the path his lips had taken on hers.

Mickey closed her eyes, moving away abruptly as a lump rose to block her throat. What was she doing? What was *he* doing?

'Not that I'm likely to,' Ryan declared drily in response to her action, and straightened his tie.

Having been drawn to look at him, for the first time Mickey noticed that he was actually wearing a suit. She had always thought he looked good in his casual clothes, but the suit fitted him perfectly and gave him an air of elegance which he wore unselfconsciously. She told herself it was ridiculous to feel proud of him, that she had no right to feel anything so possessive, but she did. That brought a tiny frown to her forehead.

'What's wrong?' he asked at once, and she realised she had been caught staring.

Mickey raised a diffident shoulder. 'I've never seen you in a suit before,' she responded rather lamely.

Mobile eyebrows rose. 'Do I pass?'

With flying colours, was her first thought, but what she actually said was, 'You'll do.' Then, to prevent him from saying more, she glanced at her watch and reached for her handbag. 'We'll be landing soon. I think I'll go and freshen up before the rush starts.'

Of course, to get out she had to brush past his legs, and she knew darned well he deliberately made it difficult for her, so that there was more contact than she had intended. Still, she got her own back by managing to step on his foot with her stiletto, before hurrying off to the toilets.

There was a hectic flush to her cheeks when she observed them in the mirror, and it had nothing to do with annoyance. To ease the heat she splashed her face with cold water. Whichever way he played it, he got to her, his accurate darts burrowing under her skin. Her hands clenched on the sink. Why had he had to be on this flight? Why did he have to be temptation with a capital T?

Her eyes held their reflection. You're weakening. Every minute you spend in his company only makes a wider breach in your defences. But it won't be long before the plane lands, and then he'll go his way and you'll go yours. This will really be the final parting. So why do you feel so desolate? It's what you want, isn't it? Isn't it?

She had to turn away, thankful that she didn't have to look in the mirror to put her hair in order. But the conversation with herself didn't make it any easier to return to her seat...and Ryan. Which only proved an anticlimax, because he wasn't there. She breathed easier, realising he had probably gone to freshen up too. There was little opportunity for talking when he did finally return, because they were soon on final approach.

Then they were on the ground and there were all the formalities of claiming luggage and going through Customs. It was then that it occurred to Mickey it might prove very awkward if Ryan was there when she met her mother. He wouldn't fail to recognise Tanita Amory, and would think it odd that she hadn't mentioned precisely who her mother was. He'd think she was ashamed, when she wasn't, but it was too late now to put matters right. She lost sight of him for a while, but her relief was short-lived, for as she was making her way to the arrivals area he caught up with her, a satirical smile hovering on his lips as he witnessed her dismay.

'I'm being met,' she told him shortly, 'so don't let me keep you.' She kept on walking, looking around for her mother, who was sure to be in the crowd somewhere. And wherever she went, publicity naturally followed. There would be nothing private about this meeting of mother and daughter, but Mickey was determined the audience would be one short.

Ryan kept pace with her easily. 'I never go anywhere I don't want to go.'

Mickey hardly found that reassuring. In exasperation she rounded on him so suddenly that he almost cannoned into her. 'What do I have to do to get you to go away?' she demanded, but was destined never to receive an answer, for over the general hubbub she heard a voice she recognised.

So did a great majority of the crowd, and after an initial lull the noise level returned greater than ever, as the human sea parted as if Moses had been present. Mickey dropped her suitcase and turned just in time to be enveloped in a crushing hug and a cloud of Chanel No. 19.

'Michaela, darling, it's so wonderful to see you at last! I've missed you so!' Tanita Amory exclaimed with unfeigned pleasure, and Mickey could do little other than return the greeting as warmly.

'I've missed you too, Mother,' she responded, ignoring the crowd with ease, yet very much aware of one pair of blue eyes glued to her back. She avoided looking Ryan's way as she eased away to take a better look at her mother.

Tanita was as beautiful as ever, and easily recognisable as the sultry beauty of countless films. Only Mickey knew what others surmised—that it was an unnatural youth, maintained by a rigid diet and the services of a discreet beauty clinic where she was regularly pinned and tucked. Tanita Amory, fading starlet, was obsessed with her disappearing looks, and, although Mickey had never had any doubt that she was loved and wanted, she had always had to compete for attention with Tanita's favourite subject—herself. This time was no different.

'Well, sweetie, how do you think your mamma looks?'

Mickey's lips curved wryly. 'You look lovely, as young as ever. I don't know how you do it.'

Tanita laughed joyfully, squeezing her arm. 'O-oh, it's so good to have you back. How on earth could I have let you stay away so long?' she declared, then gradually became aware that Mickey was not alone.

Mickey watched with a sinking feeling as her mother took in the height, breadth and style of Ryan Douglas.

There was nothing new in seeing her mother smile seductively at a personable male, but never before had she felt such anger as Tanita instinctively preened, focusing all her attention on him. She wanted to shout, Keep your eyes off him, he's mine, and unconsciously moved a step closer to him.

'You must forgive my bad manners, but it's so long since I've seen Michaela that I was quite overcome,' she now declared to Ryan, then to Mickey's horror jumped to a natural but erroneous conclusion. 'You must be Jack, Michaela's fiancé. I'm delighted to meet you at last. I swear, I was beginning to think I never would!'

Mickey closed her eyes helplessly, never having envisaged this scenario, and very much aware that in the next few seconds her mother would discover the lies she had been told. Only she was the one who received the shock. When Ryan replied, she could hardly believe her ears.

'I'm delighted to meet you too, Miss Amory. Please, call me Ryan; I've always preferred it to Jack,' he declared blithely, bending to kiss his prospective mother-in-law on both cheeks, adroitly avoiding her attempt to place one of her own on his lips.

While Mickey looked on, bemused by his nerve, her mother pouted at being thwarted. 'Ryan it is, and you must call me Tanita. I suppose you're wondering how I could possibly have a daughter old enough to be married.'

For the first time Ryan looked directly at Mickey, and the speculation in his eyes sent a shiver down her spine. Then he was smiling and pulling her stiff body into the circle of his arm. 'I should imagine it was because you married Michael Hanlon almost thirty years ago,' he drawled, then, as a dumbstruck look began to appear on Tanita's face, added, 'Perhaps you were a child bride; that's why you look more like sisters than mother and daughter.'

Tanita positively simpered. 'What a gallant thing to say. You have a very charming fiancé, darling, but you never told me he was so handsome!' she scolded gently, and never took her eyes off Ryan for a second.

Now should have been the moment to confess that there was no fiancé, but the anger she still felt towards Tanita's reaction to Ryan stopped her. She couldn't leave any man alone, and, if there was one she absolutely should avoid, then he was her daughter's fiancé! Not fully understanding all the emotions seething inside her, she still acted instinctively.

'Stop flirting with him, Mother; he's spoken for,' Mickey chided, with an edge to her voice her mother didn't miss.

Tanita's laugh was brittle. 'Don't take on so; you know I didn't mean anything by it.'

Mickey couldn't laugh, but she produced a stiff smile. She looked beyond her, expecting to see an unfamiliar face, but there was only the family chauffeur, who was well known to her. Her face registered her surprise. 'Didn't you bring your fiancé with you?'

Tanita waved an airy hand. 'Mitchell had a last-minute phone call, but he'll see you later.'

Mickey blinked. 'Mitchell? But... you can't mean Mitchell Andrews,' she gasped, recognising the name of her mother's agent, and picturing the man, who was well into his sixties and losing his hair.

For once in her life Tanita looked embarrassed. 'I know; silly, isn't it? I've known him for years. He's seen me through every disastrous marriage, and it's taken me all this time to really see him for the rock he is, and realise that it was him I loved all along!'

'I can't believe it!' Mickey replied, still dazed. Mitchell had been a constant in her own life, too, someone she could always go to for help and understanding. In fact he was the one who had agreed she was wise to leave her mother, and had been instrumental in persuading Tanita to agree.

'I can't believe it either. Oh, darling, this is like none of the others, not even your father. I feel comfortable with Mitchell. We know each other. I really do love him very much. It wasn't till we had a row and he threatened to leave that I found I couldn't face the thought of living without him. All the others I was happy to see go, but not Mitchell, and when I realised that I just knew I loved him. So simple. And being me, I had to tell him how I felt. You can't imagine how amazed I was when he told me he'd loved me for years,' she exclaimed excitedly.

Mickey looked doubtfully at her, but she had never seen her mother look so radiant. There *was* a new quality in her: an assurance and security. Suddenly she wondered if this was indeed different. Mitchell was certainly nothing like the other men she 'married', who tended to get younger as she got older. So perhaps it was his age which would prove the steadying factor. She hoped so, but those hopes were tempered by years of experience, and the knowledge that a leopard couldn't change its spots. However, she willingly gave her mother another hug.

'Let's go home, Mother. I want to meet my new step-father-to-be.'

Tanita gave her daughter a strangely relieved look, but as they moved off, it was Ryan's arm she slipped hers through with a flutter of her lashes. 'Now this isn't flirting; I'm just happier holding a gentleman's arm. You don't mind, do you, Ryan?'

He smiled down at her, and Mickey froze inside. 'Any man would be flattered to have the beautiful Tanita Amory flirt with him,' he responded, gripping tightly on to Mickey's waist when she tried to pull away. 'Come along, darling,' he urged warningly, and she was forced to keep up with them.

Her mother sighed happily. 'Mitchell is dying to meet you both,' she reported as she urged them all on, leaving the chauffeur to follow with the luggage. 'I wondered whether we should have a double wedding, but Mitchell said no. A special day deserves not to be shared, but I have hopes of persuading you to get married while you're here. As I said in my letter, two years is long enough. I don't know how either of you managed to wait so long!'

This was the sort of thing Mickey had dreaded, and she groaned inwardly. 'Mother, I——' she began, only to be interrupted.

'That's a good idea, Tanita. You'll have to let me work on Mickey.' Ryan drowned her out, and her teeth closed with a snap, leaving her unable to do more than glare at him behind her mother's back. First he flirted with her, then he took her side!

They had reached the limousine by this time, and Ryan held the door open for the two women to enter first. Mickey held back, her eyes flashing fire at him.

'What do you think you're doing? You must be out of your mind!'

'One of us is, that's for sure. This whole thing just gets more and more interesting. If your mother knows of your fiancé, then you invented him for her, not me. You used him like your words, as another handy weapon. You really must have been getting desperate!' Ryan returned in a mocking undertone, making her fume yet again.

Her chin went up. 'You are the most...'

Ryan put his hand at the small of her back and pushed her towards the car. 'If we stay out here any longer, your mother will get suspicious.'

Which, while true, hardly defused her temper. 'Don't you dare say another word!' she hissed between her teeth, before joining her mother inside.

Ryan quickly followed her in, and although there was plenty of room he deliberately chose to sit so close to her that she felt the heat of his body from thigh to shoulder. She tried to push him away surreptitiously, but he only laughed and picked up her hand, threading his fingers through hers and refusing to let go. Mickey was forced to subside or cause a scene. Things weren't going at all the way she expected, and she no longer felt in control, making her wonder just what other shocks were in store for her before this visit was over.

CHAPTER NINE

TANITA chatted the whole journey, but, while Mickey had responded at first, she grew silent as they approached the luxurious house at Antibes. It looked almost part of a fairy-tale, lit up by the last rays of the setting sun. She had grown up there, and remembered it mostly with affection, but it didn't seem real any more. Home was in British Columbia, flying her beloved planes.

She hadn't thought anyone noticed her silence, but as they entered the gates she felt Ryan's hand squeeze hers. It was strange how one small gesture could make her feel better, but it did, and she felt the tension begin to ease out of her. Confused by her reaction, she tipped her head his way, but Ryan was looking out of the window. She frowned. Had she imagined that comforting gesture? Even as she questioned it, he turned, and she knew at once that she hadn't. Yet why had he done it? And how had Ryan Douglas, of all people, picked up that brief moment of distress?

It made no sense, as so many of the things which had been happening to her lately didn't. She understood him when he was fighting her, but she felt plunged into a maze when he revealed a depth of sensitivity like just now. Unable to answer her own questions, she gave in to the small pleasure of leaving her hand in his, and unexpectedly found peace.

The moment, however, was destined to be short-lived. Tanita ushered them into the house minutes later, where they were met by the housekeeper.

'Monique, this is my daughter Michaela and her handsome fiancé Ryan. Have you prepared their room?' her mother introduced them proudly.

The housekeeper shook their hands, smiling a welcome. '*Oui, madame*. The gold room, as you requested.'

Mickey, who had been looking about her for signs of change, came to full attention as the import of that exchange sank in. *Their* room? One glance at Ryan told her he had caught the implication too, but, characteristically, he found it amusing. Mickey didn't find it at all funny. Surely to goodness her mother didn't expect them to share?

'Is Mr Andrews still in the study?'

The housekeeper shook her head. '*Non, madame*, he went out, but he will be back before dinner. Shall I show your guests upstairs?'

'No, thank you, Monique, just have Georges bring up the luggage,' Tanita refused, turning once more to her daughter. 'Come along. I've put you both in the gold room because it's nice and private,' she declared mischievously. 'And has glorious views of the coast if you're interested,' she added as she led the way upstairs.

They followed obediently, Mickey very much aware of the grip of Ryan's hand on her arm. He might have been giving a warning, but she couldn't let her mother's arrangement go past unquestioned.

She cleared her throat. 'Er—I thought you'd put me in my old room, Mother.'

Tanita laughed. 'Nonsense, darling, you know I'm no prude. You've been engaged for two years now, so how can I expect you to go back to sleeping separately?'

'But——' she began to protest, then winced to a halt as the pressure on her arm increased.

'That's very thoughtful of you, Tanita. Not all parents would be as understanding, despite their daughter's age,'

Ryan responded drily, to which her mother laughed huskily.

'Michaela will tell you I've never been a conventional parent, though I tried to do my best for her as she grew up. She never wanted for anything. Ask anyone. But she's grown up now, and I can hardly request celibacy from my daughter when I don't practise it myself. I believe in love being expressed in every way there is, and what can be more natural than sleeping together?'

As she finished speaking, she threw open the door to a room and indicated they should enter. 'Here you are. Now dinner is set for eight-thirty, with drinks beforehand. There will only be the four of us tonight, so we can get to know each other better. So you just make yourselves comfortable, and I'll see you later.' On that cheery note, she smiled warmly and left, closing the door behind her.

Neither of them moved until the sound of her footsteps had faded away, then Ryan strolled to the nearest open window and looked out.

'She was right about the view,' he observed, with more than a hint of amusement. Shrugging off his jacket, he tossed it aside with his tie and leant back against the window frame, his attention now fully on her. 'Why don't you get it off your chest before you explode?' he invited.

Mickey threw her handbag on the bed. 'Don't you dare laugh at me! None of this would have happened if you hadn't said you were my fiancé! How dared you interfere?'

'I was intrigued. Clearly your mother was expecting you to arrive with a man in tow. But as *we* both know there isn't a fiancé, that means you lied to her when you said there was. Why the lie, Hanlon?'

She was too angry to think before answering. 'To get her off the subject!' she declared, pacing angrily back and forth. 'Every letter asked me about the men in my life, and it drove me crazy. If I said there was none, she would have been worse, so I told her I was engaged. At least that narrowed the questions down to just one man!'

Ryan crossed his arms, eyes narrowed and watchful. 'Why weren't there any men?'

Mickey came to an abrupt halt at that, gasping faintly as she realised she had said too much...again. 'That's my business!'

He shrugged. 'OK, so why didn't you put Tanita right at the airport? By coming on your own, you'd obviously decided to tell her you'd lied, so why didn't you?'

Because her mother had taken one look at him and gone into her act, and she had been so angry and possessive that she'd acted without thinking! That was the truth she couldn't tell him. She licked her lips nervously and lied. 'Because you took me by surprise.'

With a shake of his head, Ryan pushed himself away from the wall and closed the distance between them. 'Oh, no, Hanlon, that just won't do. You had ample time to devise another lie. You could have said I was playing a joke, that your fiancé was sick and couldn't come. Instead you let it stand, and I know why. You wanted to be with me. You wanted an excuse to share this room with me without making the decision yourself.'

Hot colour rose into her cheeks. 'That's not true! You heard me say where I thought I'd be sleeping!' she disavowed, yet there was a niggling doubt in her mind. Had she thought that; subconsciously wanted the matter taken out of her hands?

Ryan stepped closer, taking, so it seemed to Mickey, all the available air from the room. His hands fastened on her waist, jerking her forwards until their bodies touched from chest to knee. Instantly a tide of heat engulfed her, weakening her knees and making it painful to breathe.

There were flickering fires in his eyes as she stared into them. 'That won't wash, sweetheart. You know your mother too well. You knew what she was likely to do.'

Mickey brought her hands up to his chest, but was unable to bring them to push him away. 'I—I'd forgotten. Besides, I didn't expect you to be here.' That was true; he had to admit that.

His mouth curved, and he lowered his head, pressing his lips to her throat, making her gasp aloud, and she let her head fall backwards. 'Only up to the moment I claimed to be your fiancé; then you knew. You knew exactly where it would lead,' he countered, exploring the arch of her throat with dazzling sensuality.

Mickey's lids grew heavy and she could no longer hold them open. But cutting out the light plunged her into a realm of the senses, where the feel of his caress was everything. 'Why did you say it?' she groaned out, shuddering as his tongue found a tender cord and plundered it remorselessly.

'To get close to you, of course. To get what I want from you,' he murmured huskily, trailing his lips up her throat to her cheek, searching out her mouth and hovering tantalisingly over it.

Yes, deep down she'd known that. Ever since she'd seen him on the plane, she had known this thing between them wasn't over. It had to be resolved. She ached to be close to him, but still held back, mustering pitifully weak defences in a final attempt to escape her fate. 'I won't sleep with you again, Ryan.'

He groaned deep in his throat. 'That's good, because I don't intend either of us should sleep,' he declared, and finally brought his mouth down on hers.

Mickey was swept away in an undertow of passion, unable to fight the need to respond to his highly erotic caress. Her hands slipped up around his neck, locking into his hair as she pressed herself closer to his exciting male body, feeling him stir against her with a delicious surge of feminine power. Whatever he made her feel, she made him feel too, and neither could hide it. Nor wanted to, she decided, as his hand insinuated itself beneath the jacket of her suit and found the warm bare skin of her back.

Breathlessly she tore her mouth free. 'Ryan...' She moaned his name as a kind of plea. Yet whether to stop or go on she didn't know, for Ryan abruptly moved away from her.

'Hell, you make me forget all my good intentions,' he laughed raggedly, putting the width of the room between them before he turned and faced her. 'Why didn't you tell me Tanita Amory was your mother?'

Still caught up in the spell he had woven, Mickey blinked and raised a hand to her forehead. 'What?'

Ryan shoved his hands into his trouser pockets. 'Not once on the flight did you even attempt to tell me. Why?'

Mickey finally came down to earth with a vengeance. 'I... didn't think it was important,' she muttered, regrouping her thoughts hastily. 'It isn't always easy being the daughter of someone famous, so I avoid publicity when I can. I didn't expect you to meet, so why tell you?'

Ryan studied her until she was ready to scream. 'Are you ashamed of your mother, Hanlon?'

The probing question made her furious, and she took a hasty step towards him. 'No!'

One eyebrow queried her. 'No? Are you sure about that?'

At her sides, her hands balled into fists. 'Damn you. I have never, ever been ashamed of my mother!' she protested vehemently.

Not a whit deterred by her anger, he went on, 'It would be understandable if you were, because she has quite a reputation. In fact, you could say she's notorious for her affairs.'

Mickey could feel the colour draining from her cheeks. 'I refuse to discuss my mother's love-life.'

'So you *are* ashamed of her,' Ryan declared instantly, making her see red again.

'Once and for all, will you get it into your head that I'm not ashamed of her? It's her nature; she just can't help herself. If I felt anything at all, it would be pity!' she cried, then clamped a hand over her mouth in dismay as she realised just what she had said. She'd never said that to anyone before, never even really admitted it to herself. But there was no recalling it, and no denying its truth. She stared at Ryan, and his eyes were like lasers, probing into her.

'What do you mean, "it's her nature"?'

Shaken, she turned away from him. 'Nothing.'

Ryan wasn't having that. 'If you said it, it had to mean something. Why can't she help herself?'

Feeling cornered, she rounded on him, spitting, 'What do you think I mean? You saw her yourself. Good grief, she even flirted with you!'

His eyebrows rose, then narrowed. 'I imagine she flirts with everyone.'

'Exactly,' she agreed hardily.

'What exactly are you trying to say, Hanlon?' he challenged softly, and she laughed.

'I'm not trying to say anything. I thought I was simply answering your offensive questions, thereby satisfying your pruricnt curiosity!'

To her annoyance, instead of backing off he merely smiled. 'If that's what it seems like, then you're missing the point, Hanlon. I'm not asking for my benefit, but for yours.'

'Mine?' she yelped in surprise, until slowly it dawned on her just what he meant. Something twisted painfully inside her as she looked at him. 'Oh, I get it. You want to know if I'm like my mother or not, because, if I am, then the odds are stacked in your favour, aren't they? I'm bound to fall into your bed again in the end, aren't I?' she charged scornfully, hating him.

There was a peculiar tension in his lean frame as he watched her. 'Would it be such a bad thing to end up there?' he asked her softly, and it seemed to Mickey that her heart turned over.

It would be heaven, and it would be hell. To have him would be to lose him eventually, leaving her in darkness. But to not have him at all, for even the shortest time? Wouldn't that take all the light out of the world anyway?

In the end she was saved from answering by a knock on the door. She quickly went to answer it, swallowing down a bubble of hysteria. Nothing ever went right, and she didn't know whether to be glad or sorry. The situation was intolerable and it couldn't go on. Sooner or later something was going to have to give, or she'd shatter into a thousand irretrievable pieces!

It was Georges with the luggage. As if sensing the atmosphere, he deposited the cases without a word and left. Mickey shut the door behind him, and when she turned Ryan was bending over his open case. Sensing her regard, he glanced up.

'You have the luck of the Irish, Hanlon. Saved by the bell again. But don't think this ends here; it's just postponed until we can be sure we won't be interrupted. So do you want to use the bathroom first?' he asked, as if everything was signed and settled. And wasn't it? Things had gone too far for her to demand a room of her own now, and in the back of her mind was the knowledge that he was right, she didn't want to go.

Trembling a little, she shook her head. 'No, you go. I have to unpack. I'll do yours for you if you like,' she added huskily, and he smiled.

'Very domestic, but thanks for the offer. As a mere male, I'm not likely to refuse.' He grabbed up some fresh clothes, and his smile turned wry. 'I suppose I'd be wasting my time asking you to join me. You could scrub my back, and I could scrub yours. But then I doubt we'd ever make it down to dinner. So it's another long cold shower for me. I'll try not to take too long.'

When he had gone she sank down weakly on to the dressing-table stool and put her hands to her cheeks. Staring at her reflection, she slowly came to an inevitable conclusion. It had gone too far, and there was no way back. She couldn't fight Ryan any more, but, more to the point, she couldn't fight herself. She could only be what she was, and that woman wanted him, no matter what the consequences. If it lasted a day, a week, a year, she'd accept it, and when this madness of the blood was finally over, as it surely must one day be, she would face the future head-on.

Mickey put the final touches to her make-up and surveyed the reflection in the bathroom mirror. Reflected back was a face she knew well, although there was maturity there now. But still she saw a spirited young woman who actually made her feel as if she had rediscovered a part of herself which had been sadly missing. It was quite an eye-opener. This, she realised, was her true self, and there was no getting away from it. She had laid down her arms, and, as if by magic, she felt as if an oppressive weight had been lifted from her shoulders.

She had chosen to wear one of her new dresses, a black sheath made from some clingy material. It had no shoulders, just a band of lace which cut from the top of each arm and descended to form the long, tight sleeves. She knew she looked good, and it gave an extra bounce to her walk when she emerged from the bathroom to slip on her shoes. Ryan stopped what he was doing to stare at her, and she froze, heart thudding wildly. He looked vitally handsome in black trousers and a white dinner-jacket, but what gripped her was the fire which flared to life in his eyes. It ignited one of her own which needed very little to turn into total conflagration.

'Well?' she asked huskily, and saw him swallow.

'Very well,' he confirmed, clearing his throat. 'In fact, quite a transformation, but why now?'

Her new-found acceptance made that easy to answer. 'Because nothing was going to make any difference.'

Ryan frowned slightly. 'Are you going to explain that?'

Mickey quickly shook her head. She might have made a decision, but she wasn't entirely comfortable with it yet. She felt more fatalistic than happy. 'You'll be getting the advantage of it; just be grateful. Let's go down,' she suggested, and moved towards the door.

Ryan followed her, catching her arm before she could leave. He studied the solemn face she turned to him for what seemed like an aeon before saying, 'Are you sure you want to do this?'

She laughed cynically. 'I don't have much choice. I don't suppose I ever did.'

'You're not making much sense, Hanlon,' he protested, 'but I'll go along with it for now.'

'I thought you might,' she agreed drily, and carried on out of the room.

Tanita and Mitchell were waiting for them in the lounge, and Mickey went forward to greet her prospective stepfather with a happy smile.

'It's good to see you again, Mitch. I hope you know what you're doing, marrying Mother,' she couldn't help saying as they both watched Tanita advance on Ryan and take his arm. She couldn't help stiffening angrily when he said something to make her laugh and she reached up to caress his cheek.

'Take no notice, Mickey; she just has to prove that she can attract handsome young men still,' Mitchell explained, and she frowned, looking at her mother with new eyes.

Was that all it was—a game? 'Don't you mind? You're going to marry her. Aren't you afraid she'll go off as she has before?'

Mitchell patted her hand comfortingly. 'No. She might look young, but the truth is she isn't. Her career was never spectacular, but the parts are drying up altogether, and her insecurity has got worse. So she flirts, to prove she can still attract the men, but I know she loves me. I'm her rock, and in the end she won't even have to flirt. Which is how I know your Ryan is perfectly safe, and you have no need to be jealous.'

Blushing, Mickey reached up to kiss his cheek. 'Oh, Mitch, I don't know how you put up with people like Mother and me, but I'm so glad you do.'

'So am I. Now come and introduce me to the man who's managed to win you away from your planes,' he suggested fondly, and shepherded her across the room. When they reached the other couple he let Mickey go. 'Unhand that stripling, Tanita, and come and play with someone your own age,' he ordered, and to Mickey's amazement her mother laughed, blushed, and did just that, hanging on to his arm instead.

'Don't be silly, Mitchell! Shake hands with Michaela's fiancé, Ryan.'

They shook hands, and Mitchell gave the younger man a quizzical look. 'Ryan? I thought your name was Jack,' he queried, making Mickey tense, but not Ryan.

'It's a long story. I'll tell you about it some day,' he promised, sending Mickey a conspiratorial look which brought colour to her cheeks.

Just then dinner was announced, and they all moved into the dining-room. It proved to be a lively occasion. Tanita and Mitchell were so obviously happy that it was impossible not to be affected. Mickey had not lost all her doubts, but it was true that, save for odd moments, it was her own fiancé who held her mother's attention.

She glanced across the table at Ryan. As if he was attuned to her every thought, he broke off the conversation he had been having with Mitchell to look at her. It was a look hot enough to sear her nerve-ends, and when he smiled and raised his glass to her the sip she took of her own drink was very nearly a desperate gulp. She didn't know of anyone who could make love to a woman with his eyes only, as Ryan did!

From the other end of the table, Tanita, who had watched the by-play, let out a delighted laugh, drawing everyone's attention.

'I want to make a toast. To my beautiful, precious daughter and her dashing, handsome fiancé. I wish you health, wealth, but, most of all, years and years of loving happiness!' she declared, raising her glass.

Mickey hastily lowered her eyes to where her fingers tightened on the stem of her glass. *Loving happiness? Oh, Mother, you're way off beam. This isn't true love. I've really no more idea what love is than you ever had. But passion... we both know about that. It's a kind of divine madness. I want Ryan, and he wants me. That's a form of happiness, isn't it?*

'Embarrassed, Mickey?' Mitchell asked gently, clasping his hand over hers, and bringing her head up swiftly.

Across the table, Ryan looked on thoughtfully. 'You know Mickey doesn't like being the centre of attention,' he put in quietly, bringing a look of surprise to Tanita's happy face.

'Oh, but that can't be true, Ryan. Look at all the publicity she got when the story broke of her affair with Jean-Luc. Why, she positively wallowed in it!' she insisted lightly.

Mitchell felt Mickey's hand jerk under his and squeezed it gently. 'Not everyone likes living in a goldfish bowl the way you do, darling,' he rebuked her. 'Weathering isn't the same as wallowing, you know.'

Tanita shifted uncomfortably. 'Well, I know that, but she was perfectly all right until she was cited in the divorce! That would be horrible for anyone. Especially when the man deserts you!'

Mickey pulled her hands away and dropped them into her lap, where they curled into fists. Though she knew Ryan was watching her, she refused to look at him. 'Mother, please. I'd rather not discuss it,' she said stonily.

'But darling, it was eight years ago. You can't still be sensitive about it.'

It was Ryan who came to her defence. In a gesture Mickey knew well, he raised an eyebrow questioningly. 'Why not?'

Tanita looked positively dumbfounded by the question. 'Why? Well, for heaven's sake, it was only her first affair, after all!'

Ryan didn't lose his smile, but his eyes hardened. 'That should make a difference?'

'Naturally. After that you know the rules. Every affair has a pattern. You fall in love, you fall out of love,' Tanita expanded with an amused laugh.

By this time Mickey had passed through shock at hearing Ryan champion her, and had gone on to be positively fuming. There were talking about her as if she weren't even there! Her face was a riot of colour as she looked at her mother, and something exploded inside her.

'Oh, for heaven's sake, why can't you tell the truth for once? I love you, Mother, but you know as well as I do that love had nothing to do with your affairs! Mine certainly didn't contain anything so noble!' she pronounced shortly, too angry to beat about the bush.

In the silence that fell they could all see there was a very genuine perplexity on Tanita's beautiful face. 'But of course I loved them, darling. Every single one. Maybe not the way I've just discovered I love Mitchell, but it was always love, Michaela. I would never, ever have dreamt of having a relationship with a man for any other reason! Oh, darling, I really don't understand you. What other reason could there possibly be?'

Mickey stared hard at her mother, emotions held in check for far too many years warring angrily inside her. Was Tanita's confusion genuine, or a fine piece of play-acting? Casting a look at Ryan, she found his eyes riveted on her, although there was nothing to be read from his face.

'I think we'd all be interested in the answer, Mickey,' Ryan prompted.

After all the pretence, she was suddenly deathly tired of it all. 'Sex, Mother. People have affairs just for sex!' she declared bluntly.

Her usually unshockable mother gave a tiny gasp. 'And you think I...?' She stopped and swallowed hard, her smile vanishing completely. 'I suppose it would be natural for you to see it that way when you were only a child. I never thought... Michaela, if I gave that impression, then it was purely by mistake. Oh, heavens!' she exclaimed, and turned beseeching eyes on her fiancé.

Mitchell looked quite stern. 'You're going to have to tell her, darling, because I've a notion this is very important.'

Tanita's eyes widened as she followed his glance from Ryan's tense figure to a white-faced Mickey. She smiled wanly. 'True confession time? Very well, although heaven knows what you'll think of me! Although it can't be worse than what you already imagine, can it? You have to understand I'm not a very secure person, darling. All I ever had was my talent—and that wasn't so hot—and my looks. I... I never have been much good on my own. I need the strength of a man in my life. I see now it must have seemed as if I were sex mad, and the gossip didn't help. And I guess I played up to Press, because I love being talked about, being somebody. But the truth is, despite my image, I'm not a very...passionate...woman. Bedroom games never really interested me that much. That's why the men seemed to come and go so regularly.

I tried to give them what I thought they wanted, but a creature of passion and unbridled lust I'm not.'

Mickey swayed in her seat, never for one moment having expected such a confession from her vibrant mother. 'But that can't be true!' she cried, floundering in a welter of confusion. If Tanita really wasn't the sex-kitten she had always thought she was, what, then, did it make of her?

Tanita was up on her feet in seconds, rounding the table to enclose her daughter in a hug. 'It is, but of course it's not easy for you to understand. You're such a creature of passions yourself, darling. Underneath that cool exterior you're a little volcano, just like your father. All or nothing. Either you're on a high, or in a low. Me, I just rattle along in my little groove, looking for someone to love me the way I need to be loved—gently, just as Mitchell does.'

'That would never do for Mickey,' Ryan disclosed, causing both women to look at him.

Tanita laughed. 'No, indeed. She's all fire; that's why I was so happy when she wrote and told me she was engaged. She needs someone like you, Ryan, to keep the pot boiling. She'll never be happy unless it is. Like her father, if there isn't an argument brewing, she'll make one, just to enjoy the fun of making up afterwards. Jean-Luc was all wrong, but she never would have listened to me had I said so. Headstrong. But, as I said, all or nothing. She needs someone who understands that. Fortunately I took one look at you and knew you were perfect!'

Ryan grinned wryly. 'I'm glad to hear it. Now all I have to do is get Mickey to agree with you,' he added, dropping his gaze to link with Mickey's startled one.

'Doesn't she?' Mitchell asked in some concern.

'Not always, but the times she does make up for all the others,' he replied softly.

Mickey couldn't laugh the way the others did. There was a tension gripping her which made her feel as if her head would explode if she didn't get away on her own. Abruptly she pushed her chair back and sprang to her feet.

'I'm sorry, but you'll have to excuse me,' she declared brokenly, and, without giving anyone time to stop her, fled from the room.

CHAPTER TEN

HALFWAY up the stairs a vice-like hand fastened on her arm and forced her to slow down. Turning her ashen face towards Ryan, she attempted to pull herself free without success.

'Will you please let me go? I want to be alone,' she demanded stiffly.

Ryan didn't even miss a step. 'It might be what you want, but it sure as hell isn't what you need,' he contradicted lightly.

Mickey gnashed her teeth in impotent fury. 'How do you know what I need?' Damn it, he was always laying down the law!

He spared her a glance, one bereft of even the slightest mockery. 'Because I know you better than you know yourself, darling.' Then almost to himself he added, 'The trouble starts when you begin to realise your power.'

She drew in her breath sharply. 'What does that mean?'

His smile was dry. 'Don't expect me to hand you any more weapons than you have, Hanlon.'

'I don't have any weapons at all!' Mickey protested as they reached their room and he threw the door open, ushering her in ahead of him before closing and locking it firmly.

Only then did Ryan throw back his head and laugh. 'You've an arsenal which would make the Russians envious,' he countered as he released her.

Mickey took the opportunity to put the width of the room between them. 'Right now I don't want to make anyone envious. I just want to be left in peace.'

Removing his jacket, Ryan draped it over a chair and unfastened his bow-tie and several shirt buttons. 'Hanlon, there will be no peace between us ever, at least not a lasting one, and if you're honest you'll admit you don't want one. What we have is far more exciting,' he told her, not troubling to close the gap, and in consequence making her feel more under threat than ever.

'We have nothing,' she denied.

'Only because you're too afraid to admit it.'

Her mouth went dry. What was he trying to make her say now? That she wanted him? Well, he already knew that. She gave herself away every time they touched.

'I'm not afraid of anything.'

'Only yourself.'

Her heart jolted, because it was true . . . had been true. But she had already decided she was no longer going to deny she wanted to go to bed with him again, so why did she suddenly feel so threatened? Yet as ever, when under threat, she came out fighting.

'Not so. If you want me to say I want to make love with you, then I'll say it. OK, you win; I'll go to bed with you.'

If she had expected him to show triumph, she was disappointed. If anything he tensed rather than relaxed. 'Sorry, Hanlon, but that option is no longer on offer.'

Following so closely on the revelations downstairs, that was a body-blow, and Mickey rocked back on her heels. 'What?'

Now he did walk towards her, and, taking her by the shoulders, steered her to the bed and pushed her down so that she was sitting on the end of it. 'There's only one deal on offer this time, Hanlon, and that relies on how you answer the questions I'm going to put to you.'

He had just pulled the rug out from under her, and she didn't seem to know which way was up any more. She couldn't seem to take her eyes away from his. She had never heard him sound so serious. 'What questions?' she asked gruffly.

To her surprise Ryan didn't sit beside her, but walked across to the window and stood with his back to her, staring out into the darkness. 'First I want you to tell me about your affair with Jean-Luc.'

Her breath caught in her throat. Always before she had refused, but the events of the day had taken the fight from her. There really didn't seem much point in keeping it to herself any more. 'What do you want to know?'

'Everything, from beginning to end.'

Mickey sighed heavily. 'There's not much to tell really. He was a power-boat racer. I'd never met anyone like him. He was handsome and exciting, and the moment I saw him I wanted him. I thought it was so romantic, meeting in secret, making forbidden love...' She broke off, reaching the crux of the matter. 'Then his wife found out, and threatened to divorce him, and he went back to her. He told me that although I was a sexy little thing he wasn't about to lose her for the sake of a roll in the hay with me!' she finished harshly, and jumped violently when Ryan picked up a vase and threw it against the wall, where it smashed to smithereens.

'The bastard!' he swore, and there was a white line of anger about his mouth as he glanced at her. 'He didn't tell you he was married?'

'No, but I should have guessed,' she said shakily, vaguely alarmed by his anger.

Ryan wasn't about to accept that. 'Don't defend the snake, Hanlon. He was a married man with a wealth of experience, and you were a rather naïve teenager. He knew exactly what he was doing when he made you fall in love with him!'

Her colour rose. 'I didn't fall in love with him!'

'What was it, then?'

Damn him! 'Sex! It was just sex! He sent everything out of my mind except the way he could make me feel!'

Ryan seemed to freeze, and chose his words carefully. 'The way I do?'

Shock made her pale. 'No!' Her denial was instant and vehement, surprising her, because up until that moment she had believed utterly that sex was precisely what it was. Apparently she hadn't surprised Ryan.

'But isn't that what you're afraid of, Hanlon? That you want me, just as you wanted him, and that it's just sex?' he probed on, making her heart thunder in her chest.

Emotions threatened to burst her wide open, and she clamped her hands over her ears. 'Stop it!'

In an instant he was before her, crouching down, pulling her hands away, forcing her to hear him. 'Isn't it true, Hanlon, that for the last eight years you've imagined yourself to be some sort of raving nympho?'

All the fight went out of her as if someone had pulled the plug. He knew. He knew everything, and she felt as if she stood naked before him. There was no point in lying. She had the feeling he would see right through it. She swallowed hard, trying to moisten an arid throat. 'How did you know?'

'I'd half guessed for some time, but today finally brought it all together.'

'So that's why you changed your mind about going to bed with me?'

He watched her soberly, shaking his head. 'I still want that, but it comes with strings, I'm afraid.'

Mickey closed her eyes, not understanding anything. 'But I thought——'

'That because you had the misfortune to fall in love with a man who used that love to slake his own lust I'd no longer want you?' he finished for her, putting a hand beneath her chin and forcing her to look at him.

She flushed, not knowing where this was going, but, having got this far, she had to go on, whatever it made him think of her. 'It wasn't love. It was lust. I wanted him, so I had him. I behaved just like...just like...' The words choked in her throat.

Ryan muttered something harsh under his breath. 'Listen to me, Hanlon,' he growled, shaking her. 'It was love you felt. You had a passionate nature you didn't understand, and you were used by a man who did. You couldn't have been behaving like your mother, because she's just got through telling you she doesn't have a high sex drive. The only mistake you made was falling for a guy who didn't deserve your love. For the past eight years you've been punishing yourself for sins you never even committed.'

Dazed, Mickey finally recognised the truth when she heard it. Put like that, it was so obvious that she wondered how she could have been blind for so long. But she had been young, and very naïve, despite her upbringing. She hadn't understood herself at all, and was only slowly coming to do so now. An excruciating wave of embarrassment flooded her, so that she could barely look at him.

'You must think I'm a fool. I thought it was love I felt, but when he left I realised it wasn't. The only role model I had to go by was my mother, and, because I believed what I did of her, I was so certain I was only capable of lust,' Mickey revealed, wincing as the words finally saw the light of day.

In response, Ryan threw his head back and swore at the ceiling. 'Didn't it ever occur to you once to doubt that conclusion? Not once in eight years?'

Mickey lifted a diffident shoulder. 'I was too busy making sure it never happened again. I thought if I put temptation out of the way, then I wouldn't be tempted.'

Ryan closed his eyes briefly before regarding her solemnly, although his eyes danced with amusement.

'You're unbelievable! Hell, anyone with a passion for sex as you describe would be hard pushed to remain celibate for a week, let alone eight years! Didn't that thought ever enter your crazy head? No, don't tell me; you just thought you had good self-control, right?'

She went from embarrassment to anger in one jump. 'Don't you laugh at me, Ryan!' she ordered, wincing now at the self-evident fact that it hadn't been hard to say no, because nobody had come close to tempting her to say yes. It hadn't been a struggle at all until Ryan had come along. Ryan! In an instant hot colour rose into her cheeks and confusion returned.

Ryan hadn't taken his eyes off her for a second, and now he watched her colour rise with interest. 'Just occurred to you, has it, Hanlon, that eight years of celibacy went out the window the minute I turned up on your doorstep? What conclusion have you come to?'

Taunted beyond bearing, Mickey glowered at him. 'I'd rather hear your no doubt fascinating idea first. Come on, Ryan, what's your explanation?' she jeered, ready to hit him if he made one more joke.

If he read the threat in her eyes, he ignored it. 'Hell, Hanlon, that's the easiest thing to explain. You love me.'

There was a moment when she remained in shock, then the next she pulled away from him and rose jerkily to her feet. 'Don't be silly; I can't love you!' Love him? That was totally out of the question!

With a long-suffering sigh, Ryan straightened up. 'Why not?'

Her mind went blank, and it was suddenly impossible to think of a single reason. 'Because...' she insisted lamely.

There was a mocking twist to the raising of his eyebrow. 'Oh, very intelligent, very lucid,' he taunted softly. 'Can't you do better than that? Aren't you going to tell me it's because you aren't capable of love, only lust? But we've just consigned that old idea to the scrap-heap, so what else is there?'

Mickey felt an exhilarating rush of blood to her cheeks as anger surged. 'OK, so what if we have? What if I got it all wrong? That still doesn't mean I love you!' she pointed out quickly.

Ryan hitched his hands on his hips and regarded her thoughtfully, not missing the tell-tale signs of annoyance. They seemed to amuse him. 'I think it does, or else why is it me alone who turned you on after eight years?' he countered.

Mickey's hands clenched into fists at her sides. Why was he persisting in this, when there was no point to it? No point at all. 'Perhaps I just got frustrated!' she snapped, so churned up inside that it was difficult to think at all.

He laughed outright. 'Believe me, Hanlon, you don't know what frustration is! I've had a bellyful of it since I met you,' he shot right back. 'But we were talking about love, not frustration. Ask yourself this. If I were seriously injured, would you care?'

Mickey closed her eyes briefly. Well, of course she would care; she wasn't callous and unfeeling! However, that didn't make it love! 'What is this—twenty questions?'

There was a sardonic twist to his smile. 'Afraid to answer, sweetheart?'

Her chin rose immediately. 'No. The answer is I'd care about anyone who was seriously injured.'

Ryan rubbed his finger along the side of his nose. 'OK, that wasn't personal enough, so try this. How would you feel at the thought of me making love to somebody else?'

Something like a red-hot poker speared through her heart. That really hit home. She found she could actually visualise him in another woman's arms, and the picture brought nausea to her throat. She'd want to kill

him, tear him to shreds for betraying her. He was hers,
damn it! That revealing reaction shocked her so much
that she couldn't have answered for the life of her.

He didn't seem to need one; a look at her face was
enough. 'Something tells me never to try it if I want to
remain alive!' he declared drily. 'All right, Hanlon, last
question, and think carefully before you answer. If I were
to tell you I was going to walk out that door and you
would never see me again, would you just let me go?'

He might just as well have run over her with a steam-
roller, for the effect was the same. She felt flattened.
Oh, God, never see him again? It would be a living death.
It would be to see her happiness vanish, and along with
it all her reasons for living! How could she ever just let
him go? She loved him too much!

Stunned, she swayed where she stood. Loved him?
Wondrously she explored the idea, realising she had been
resisting the obvious. Of course she loved him. It was
the only answer which explained all those inexplicable
things she had been experiencing since the first moment
she met him. Acceptance made her heart seem to swell
in her chest, only stopping when an icy finger ran down
he spine.

She might have finally discovered the truth about
herself, but what good did it do her? Not once this
evening had Ryan mentioned loving her. Even when he
had begun this examination of her feelings he had made
no mention of his own. She knew he wanted her, but
that wasn't love either. All the pain he had ever made
her feel coalesced into an agony of the heart.

Dear lord, what cruel game was he playing? He had
guessed she loved him, and made her admit it to
herself . . . but why? Why had he done it? What was his
purpose? She looked at him. He was expecting an answer,
and she had to give him one. Not the truth, though. Not
for the sake of a game whose rules she didn't understand.

'What are you trying to prove, Ryan, and why prove it at all? What difference does it make whether I love you or not? Let's be honest; you want me to go to bed with you, you don't want me to love you,' she said tautly.

For a moment Ryan did no more than return her gaze squarely, then he gave the oddest laugh and said, 'Honesty,' in a tone she had never heard before. Then he came to her, cupping her face in his hands before she had the chance to move away, and keeping her there with the sheer tenderness of his touch. 'Actually, Hanlon,' he admitted huskily, 'I've never wanted anything so much in my whole life as having you love me the way I love you.'

Mickey heard the words, and although they were the very ones her heart had wanted to hear something exploded in her head. 'I don't believe you! Why the hell should I? You've put me through an emotional wringer, and now you calmly expect me to accept that you love me! How can you do that?' she cried, thumping one fist against his solid chest angrily, even as she felt she was on the verge of tears. It was too much!

Ryan's face twisted with self-mockery. 'Crazy as it may seem, darling, I don't have much choice in the matter. You see, I happen to have fallen in love with you the moment I saw you!' he confessed.

She went absolutely still. 'No!' she denied, even as her body began to tremble.

'Very much yes.'

She had to be going insane. This couldn't really be happening. 'You laughed at me!' How she remembered the moment.

Ryan's smile softened achingly. 'Ah, Mickey, what else could I do when I'd just been dealt a mortal blow?'

Daft as it might seem, it was the use of her name, spoken like a caress, which undermined her resistance. As if by magic the shaking stopped, and a slow warmth began to rise in her as the willingness to believe took hold. 'You fought me at every step!' she accused in a wobbly voice, not quite ready to capitulate totally.

The tension in him subsided as something in her words and manner delivered a subliminal message. With a heartfelt groan he shook his head in disbelief. 'Oh, boy, did I ever fight you! I thought I was fighting for my life, until I realised I fought because I enjoyed the way you fought back. To be at war with you, Hanlon, is the most intoxicating experience, only capped by having you in my arms.'

The heat that that confession brought to his eyes made her shiver, and she hastily dropped her lids lest he should see her instantaneous response. For with every word he spoke, something wonderful was happening to her. Every single atom of her was coming joyously alive, swelling with the knowledge that he loved her. Ryan Douglas loved her! And she wanted to savour it, stretch it out until it encompassed her entirely, leaving no part of her aching with loneliness.

There was just the hint of a curve to her lips as she brought her other hand up to his chest and fiddled with a button. 'Go on,' she urged softly, and heard his sharp intake of breath just before her head was tipped up for his inspection.

She witnessed for herself the shock of understanding which rippled across his face before it softened sensually. 'Go on? Do I have reason to? Wouldn't this be the time to tell me the truth? Would you deny a hungry man sustenance, a thirsty man wine?'

Mickey blinked limpid eyes, knowing exactly what he wanted to hear. But he had put her through a wringer and she needed to exact revenge. 'But not ten minutes ago it was you who told me how I felt.'

She had expected him to laugh, but he didn't. Instead his face became taut. 'Don't play with my heart, Mickey, unless you want to see it broken. *Is* that what you want?

Have I pushed too hard trying to make you reveal the real you?'

It was then she made a discovery. He was afraid. The proud, self-confident Ryan Douglas was afraid that he had hurt her too much! Shock quickly gave way to dismay, and without hesitation her hands slipped up around his neck as she pressed her body close to his.

'Oh, don't ever think that! I love you, Ryan. I think I've always loved you, but I was too mixed up to see it. You made me think straight for the first time in eight years. If you're crazy enough to love a crazy woman, I'm just going to take advantage of it.'

There was an instant when Ryan's arms held her rib-crushingly close, then he eased her away and rested his forehead on hers. 'I've a better idea. Why don't you take advantage of me instead?' he invited in a voice which curdled her insides and set nerves tingling and pulses throbbing.

Mickey bit her lip and cast a look up through her lashes, senses leaping at the scorching heat in his eyes. 'You mean take you to bed?' she queried huskily, legs turning to mush as his hands glided down her spine to settle on her hips.

He laughed, but to her delight it was a little off-key. 'I thought you'd never ask,' he growled, and lowered his lips to her bare shoulder, tasting her scented skin in a series of teasing kisses which led up towards her ear.

Her fingers curled into his shirt. 'I did, but you told me there were strings,' she reminded him, gasping as he found her ear and his tongue began to explore the shell-like convolutions.

Her words caused him to stop and ease away to look right at her. 'Hell, you're a hard woman, Hanlon. No pay, no play, hmm?'

Mickey's eyes dropped to his mouth, and her breath caught in her throat as she fought the urge to cover it with her own. 'Your rules, not mine.'

Ryan pulled a face and closed his eyes. 'I should have kept my mouth shut. It's just occurred to me you could say no.'

'Am I likely to?'

He groaned. 'You're likely to do anything; that's why I love you so much. But it doesn't increase my confidence,' he told her gruffly, before he took a deep breath. 'Hell, what can I lose, except my sanity? The strings are simple, darling. You have to agree to marry me before I get in that bed with you.'

Slowly her lips parted in a smile, which swelled the look of love in her eyes. 'And to think none of this would ever have happened if the fates hadn't made you take the same flight as me!' she declared wonderingly.

Ryan froze. 'Ah.'

Green eyes quartered blue ones. 'Ah?'

'Well, actually, darling, fate had nothing to do with it. Leah told me which flight you would be on, and I made sure I had a seat on it,' Ryan confessed.

'Leah?'

In answer Ryan swung her up in his arms and carried her to the bed, where he sat down with her on his lap. 'Sweetheart, I'm no different from any other man. I was in love with you, but getting nowhere. I had to talk to someone, and Leah was there. When she knew how I felt about you she promised to help me. I'm afraid we plotted it together. You see, I felt I needed to meet your mother, that she was involved somehow, and I could only do that here. Being taken as your fiancé was a bonus.'

Mickey nestled her head into his shoulder and sighed. 'So Leah knew, and Sophie knew. Even Sid guessed. The only person who didn't know I loved you was me.'

His large hand cupped her face gently and tipped her head up. 'Oh, you knew, Mickey; you just got your wires crossed. Am I forgiven?'

She pouted, enjoying stringing the moment out. 'I shouldn't. When you left like that I was hurt. I believed you couldn't possibly be serious about me, that I was just a brief fling.'

Ryan traced his thumb over her lips, smoothing them into a sensual curve. 'Whereas you were everything, and I wouldn't have gone if I hadn't got commitments.'

Mickey's eyes widened with compunction. 'I forgot to ask you how Bobby was,' she exclaimed contritely, and he smiled.

'Bobby's fine, recovering nicely. And how are you?'

'What do you mean, how am I?' She frowned back in confusion.

Ryan toyed with a lock of her hair. 'Well, it occurred to me that you might be pregnant.'

'Pregnant?'

'Don't sound so surprised. It could have happened. Neither of us took precautions, did we?' he charged, and she flushed. 'Anyway, it gave me a legitimate excuse to come after you. Only it turned out I didn't need it when your mother mistook me for your fiancé.'

'Would you have come without an excuse?'

Now he grinned. 'Nothing would have kept me away, but I needed something which would make you accept having me round you. I reasoned I'd have a few weeks to make you realise how you really felt about me. I would never have left, only I had to get away to do some serious planning and thinking. It isn't easy to do with you around.'

'Do I drive you crazy, Ryan?'

'In more ways than one, you little devil!' he admitted with a growl, but his eyes sent her an altogether different message. One which set her heart thumping wildly.

'I like the sound of that. So I'd better forgive you, and agree to marry you,' she murmured silkily, rubbing herself against him like a cat. 'Now what do we do?'

Ryan's teeth flashed whitely as he pushed her backwards on to the bed and pinned her there with his body. 'Now, my green-eyed little witch, we settle an old score, and I can't wait,' he informed her, and took her mouth.

Mickey's instinctive query died beneath his lips, and she sighed, forgetting everything except the delicious pleasure kissing him afforded her. Given free rein at last, her hands traced the undulations of his broad back, then, impatient at being kept at a distance, tugged his shirt free and closed on warm male flesh. Her roving fingers traced his spine as Ryan's lips trailed a heated path down her throat. She didn't feel him free the zip of her dress, only the brush of air on her skin as he peeled it away from her to allow his lips to find the valley of her breasts.

He raised his head as his hand glided up to cup the swelling bounty, her nipples already aroused and erect. A finger flicked out, and she gasped, arching her back, willing him to touch her, needing it. For one soul-searching moment he locked his eyes with hers, then with infinite slowness lowered his head and took her into his mouth. She cried out as pleasure speared its way to her loins, starting up an ache which each stroke of his tongue increased. Her fingers curled into his back as he left her, but it was only to shift his attention to the twin globe and inflict the same delicious torture there.

Her breathing was ragged when he finally lifted his head again, and she watched languorously as he drew her dress away from her, tossing it on to the floor before removing the small triangle of silk which was her sole remaining covering. The heat in his eyes made her feel deliciously wanton, but not ashamed.

'You're beautiful, Mickey,' he murmured thickly as he stood up and removed his own clothes.

When he stood before her, tall and golden, and magnificently aroused, her heart leapt.

'I love you,' she told him, and held out her hand, rising to meet him as he knelt on the side of the bed,

pressing her face into the silken hair of his chest and
breathing him in. Her lips sought his male nipples,
finding them hard like her own, and hearing him catch
his breath and latch his fingers into her hair as she teased
them.

Framing her head with his hands, he urged her to her
knees, taking her mouth in a kiss so deeply erotic that
she could do no more than cling to him as she went
molten inside. Like putting a match to tinder, the first
flickering became a blaze. Passion held too long in check
burst the bounds they had used to constrain it, and con-
sumed them. They toppled sideways, mouths clinging,
arms and legs entwined.

Ryan was such a strong man that Mickey was en-
thralled by his tenderness. The glide of his palm across
her skin as he sought to know all of her was like a lick
of flame. She fell back as he claimed her breasts once
more, suckling deeply on the engorged flesh while he
sought the feminine core of her. She could feel the coil
of tension building inside her, but was unable to halt it,
riding the small explosions of pleasure until they subsided, leaving her gasping but unfulfilled.

When Ryan raised himself to look at her she stared
at him in disappointment. 'I wanted you with me,' she
protested, and he smiled and softly kissed her.

'I will be, darling, but this time I had to settle a score.'

'What score?' she breathed, knowing he was teasing
her, knowing there was more and better to come.

His hand curved possessively around her breast. 'I had
to prove I'm not an animal.'

Mickey gasped, recalling what she had said. 'No,
you're not an animal, but you are a beast. You'll pay
for that, Ryan Douglas,' she declared, and proceeded to
make him do so in the only way she knew how.

Pushing him on to his back, she took delight in doing
to him what he had done to her, savouring his moans
and sighs of pleasure. But he was stronger than her, and

when she would have taken him to the limit he swiftly turned the tables on her and rolled over to pin her beneath him. They were both breathing raggedly, barely holding on to a precarious control. Then he kissed her, and there was no going back. Mickey arched into him as he entered her, loving the feel of him within her, finding his rhythm and matching it, urging him on as a coil of tension spiralled out of control. With a cry she felt herself plunge over the edge, then seconds later Ryan joined her, and she clung to him as the world faded, leaving her floating on a cloud of utter fulfillment.

It was a long while before the real world impinged itself on her consciousness, and she was reluctant to join it, until she opened heavy lids and discovered Ryan gazing down at her.

'Hi,' he greeted huskily, brushing the damp hair from her forehead with faintly trembling fingers.

She smiled lazily. 'Hi, yourself.'

'Good?'

'Very good,' she agreed, capturing his hand and bringing it down so that she could kiss it.

A wicked grin spread across his face. 'And you said nothing good could ever come from me!' he scoffed.

Mickey couldn't help but laugh. 'Have you remembered everything I said?'

'You attacked my manhood; what else do you expect?'

She pinched him playfully. 'I'll have to remember you've got a fragile ego. OK, I'll admit I was wrong if you explain something. You've been calling me Mickey, not Hanlon; why?'

Blue eyes took on a tender gleam. 'Because you're Mickey to me when I'm making love to you, but when we fight you'll always be Hanlon. And we will fight; your mother was right about that,' he told her gently.

Mickey liked the sound of having two names; it made her feel special.

'By the way, I'll be needing a good pilot to get me to all the sites for my next commission. Can you recommend one?' Ryan ventured as he turned on to his back and tucked his hands beneath his head.

Mickey came up on her elbow to squint down at him. When he failed to meet her eyes she knew something was in the wind. 'Adam's my best pilot. He's ex-Air Force,' she offered.

'Sorry, Adam will be too busy helping Sid run Hanlon Air. Think again,' he told her, making her eyes widen.

'Oh, yes?' she challenged, the light of battle igniting in her eyes.

Ryan doused it with a few well chosen words. 'I want you with me, Hanlon. I *need* you with me. When we're home I'd be only too happy to help you with your company, but I want you with me when I have to go away,' he pronounced gruffly, and her throat closed over.

How could she argue? He was offering her the best of both worlds. He made her feel loved and needed, and, if truth be told, she didn't want to be apart from him either.

'OK,' she agreed, not finding it at all difficult to think of handing over the reins.

'No argument?'

Mickey traced the dimple in his chin. 'Don't get too confident; you won't always get your own way,' she cautioned, then her eyes dropped to his smiling mouth mere inches away and she quickly kissed him twice. When he looked a question, she laughed. 'I remember things too. That's for the two photographs you took. Now can I have them back?'

His answer was to pull her head down until he was speaking against her lips. 'Sorry, sweetheart, but the interest just went sky-high. However, if you start now, you might just have paid for them in about fifty years.'

'Ryan Douglas, you're the most...' Her protest died under his lips, and she sighed, all thought of photographs vanishing on the breeze.

SUMMER SPECIAL!

Four exciting new Romances for the price of three

Each Romance features British heroines and their encounters with dark and desirable Mediterranean men. *Plus, a free Elmlea recipe booklet inside every pack.*

So sit back and enjoy your sumptuous summer reading pack and indulge yourself with the free Elmlea recipe ideas.

Available July 1994   Price £5.70

MILLS & BOON

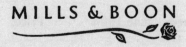

Available from WH Smith, John Menzies, Volume One, Forbuoys, Martins, Woolworths, Tesco, Asda, Safeway and other paperback stockists. Also available from Mills & Boon Reader Service, FREEPOST, PO Box 236, Croydon, Surrey CR9 9EL. (UK Postage & Packing free)

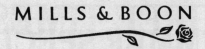

MILLS & BOON

Proudly present...

CHARLOTTE LAMB'S

♥ *100th* ♥

ROMANCE

This is a remarkable achievement for a writer who had her
first Mills & Boon novel published in 1973. Some six million
words later and with sales around the world, her novels
continue to be popular with romance fans everywhere.

Her centenary romance '*VAMPIRE LOVER*' is a suspense-
filled story of dark desires and tangled emotions—Charlotte
Lamb at her very best.

Published: June 1994   **Price: £1.90**

*Available from WH Smith, John Menzies, Volume One, Forbuoys, Martins,
Woolworths, Tesco, Asda, Safeway and other paperback stockists.
Also available from Mills & Boon Reader Service, FREEPOST,
PO Box 236, Croydon, Surrey CR9 9EL (UK Postage & Packing free).*

THREE TIMES
A LOVE STORY

A special collection of
three individual love
stories from one of
the world's best-loved
romance authors.
This beautiful volume
offers a unique
chance for new fans
to sample some of
Janet Dailey's earlier
works and for long-
time fans to collect an
edition to treasure.

W🌑RLDWIDE

AVAILABLE NOW   PRICED £4.99

Available from WH Smith, John Menzies, Volume One, Forbuoys, Martins,
Woolworths, Tesco, Asda, Safeway and other paperback stockists.
Also available from Worldwide Reader Service, FREEPOST,
PO Box 236, Croydon, Surrey CR9 9EL. (UK Postage & Packing free)

Accept 4 FREE Romances and 2 FREE gifts

FROM READER SERVICE

Here's an irresistible invitation from Mills & Boon. Please accept our offer of 4 FREE Romances, a CUDDLY TEDDY and a special MYSTERY GIFT! Then, if you choose, go on to enjoy 6 captivating Romances every month for just £1.90 each, postage and packing FREE. Plus our FREE Newsletter with author news, competitions and much more.

Send the coupon below to: Mills & Boon Reader Service, FREEPOST, PO Box 236, Croydon, Surrey CR9 9EL.

NO STAMP REQUIRED

Yes! Please rush me 4 FREE Romances and 2 FREE gifts! Please also reserve me a Reader Service subscription. If I decide to subscribe I can look forward to receiving 6 brand new Romances for just £11.40 each month, post and packing FREE. If I decide not to subscribe I shall write to you within 10 days - I can keep the free books and gifts whatever I choose. I may cancel or suspend my subscription at any time. I am over 18 years of age.

Ms/Mrs/Miss/Mr _____ EP70R

Address _____

_____

Postcode _____ Signature _____

Offer closes 31st October 1994. The right is reserved to refuse an application and change the terms of this offer. One application per household. Offer not valid for current subscribers to this series. Valid in UK and Eire only. Overseas readers please write for details. Southern Africa write to IBS Private Bag X3010, Randburg 2125. You may be mailed with offers from other reputable companies as a result of this application. Please tick box if you would prefer not to receive such offers ☐

mps MAILING PREFERENCE SERVICE